SHOOTING
THE WIRE

First published in 2019
by Eyewear Publishing Ltd
Suite 333, 19-21 Crawford Street
London, W1H 1PJ
United Kingdom

Graphic design by Edwin Smet
Author photograph by Judi MacNeil
Cover image Getty Images, antonioiacobelli
Printed in England by TJ International Ltd, Padstow, Cornwall

The editor has generally followed American spelling and punctuation at the author's request.

Set in Bembo 13 / 17 pt
ISBN 978-1-912477-83-8

WWW.EYEWEARPUBLISHING.COM

SHOOTING THE WIRE

A NOVEL

ROBERT D. KIRVEL

EYEWEAR PUBLISHING

Robert D. Kirvel
holds a Ph.D. in neuropsychology and
is a two-time Pushcart Prize and Best of the Net
nominee for fiction. In addition to winning the
Chautauqua 2017 Editor's Prize for an essay on growing
up gay in the United States and United Kingdom, he was
awarded the 2016 Fulton Prize for the Short Story and a
2015 ArtPrize for creative nonfiction. He has published
stories or essays in England, New Zealand, Ireland,
Germany, and Canada; in translation and anthologies;
and in dozens of U.S. literary journals. Chapters in this
book selected as finalists for awards include "BioYou"
for the *Eastern Iowa Review* Experimental Fiction Prize
and "Shooting the Wire" for *The Indianola Review* Flash
Fiction Prize. *Shooting the Wire*, the novel, was shortlisted
for the *Wordrunner* eChapbooks competition and was a
finalist for the *Quarterly West* Novella Contest as well as
Eyewear Publishing's 2016 Beverly Prize. The author lives
in the culturally diverse San Francisco Bay Area, except
when he communes with grizzly bears and other critters
at his Montana cabin overlooking the Livingston
Range of Glacier-Waterton International Peace
Park. Links to most of his literary publications
are at twitter.com@Rkirvel.

To my mother for her encouragement,
my father who championed education, and
Norm Estes who never took a savior into his heart.

PRINCIPAL CHARACTERS

TED
A 45-year-old family man

LAVINIA
Ted's attractive wife

THEIR DAUGHTER
A struggling artist

SID
Ted's uncle

SARAH
Ted's aunt

CLIFFORD
Sid and Sarah's son

TED'S FATHER
A Mahler enthusiast

TED'S MOTHER
A big spender

GENE AND SHIRLEY
Ted's brother and sister-in-law

THEIR OLDEST SON
A gun lover

EXERCISE YOURSELF THEN IN WHAT LIES IN YOUR POWER

– Epictetus, *The Manual*

PART ONE

I. TED

She claims she used to watch him die three, maybe four, times a day. I believe her. Studying a rise and fall of the chest until, sometimes, motion ceased and he turned blue, she'd hold her breath. Ten seconds. Twenty. Three physicians offered one opinion. Periodic breathing, they labeled it, or central sleep apnea. Nothing obstructive, so probably not much to worry about. That was then.

Selecting the leather chair, she fumbles now with her designer handbag to pull out the latest iteration of smartphone. She might be switching settings to silent mode or checking for messages. I don't ask. The phone slides back into the purse as she tickles the hem of a pencil skirt then tugs costly fabric a millimeter down a leg, silky and lean for the mother of a thirty-something son, plus two much-younger children.

"The Saturday paper reported on a man who killed his wife and children." Her breath catches before a lengthy exhalation down a country lane. A stroll of remembrance. "Then himself. With a gun. Did you see?"

I nod once, catching the staccato cadence, and wait.

"On the front page. Out of nowhere."

She leans my way as if about to thump sense into the desk but does not touch it, dialing down the usual in-your-face theatrics. Black hair spills and is tossed back as a swimmer might do after a dip. Tangle-free treatment with salon product guaranteed to glow.

"All the relatives and neighbors said the same about how he was the last person on the planet who could do such a thing. An upscale, rural community with five acres of property and a good job. Money. Can you imagine? Not a problem. Do you see?"

"I see," I say.

"My memories."

"How's that?"

"As a girl listening to adults spout advice, I used to have this temptation in the back of my mind. I don't know where it came from, but I couldn't stop it. I could see myself getting right in the person's face and saying the most abrasive thing out loud no matter what. I didn't care though. Cut to the quick." A hint of color blooms on Shirley's cheeks, the afterglow of spent rocket fuel.

I offer something noncommittal. "When you were a young person."

She sits back and re-straightens the hem that did not ask for adjustment the first time. "Well no, not exactly."

My eyebrow is uplifted, but I say nothing.

"I still feel the urge, of course. But the point is, I don't do it. I don't speak my mind or respond rudely to people, I mean, even if I don't like what they're talking about and think it ignorant. I hold back as any mature person does."

An invocation of restraint for good reason. I do not

say it but remember visiting an exhibition of impression-ist masterworks hung along a museum wall. A patron re-mains motionless while studying a Degas. The painting is blues and yellows, and the woman in the museum is dressed in a tailored outfit much like the one my sister-in-law wears today. A multicolored scarf drapes neck and shoulders. I stand behind her as if a lover and feel my arm move forward as of its own accord, and in imagination I see the hand – my own, yet somehow not my hand – reach out to grasp her scarf as if she were a familiar, then tug. Pull it away, revealing ivory shoulders.

"Everyone feels the urge," I say.

"Do they?" Her question sounds more like disagree-ment.

"Everybody at one time or another imagines acting on impulse. As a kid, when the family went to a movie theatre downtown or an auditorium, the circus say, my dad always took us up to the balcony. Front row if pos-sible. Even if the orchestra section were half empty, he thought we had better views from balcony seats. I hated it."

"What are you talking about, Ted?"

"I was terrified by an image boiling in my head of go-ing over the edge. I could feel myself trying to brace back but leaning forward instead as if captive to some invisible force pulling me over the brink. I could feel the physical draw. To this day I avoid balconies."

I decide that's enough said because two things are obvious. The conversation is not about some milquetoast family guy from a semi-bucolic neighborhood who murders his wife and children out of the blue. What Shirley is saying is not about Shirley's imagined inclination to restraint. It is about someone else.

I picture him. A pika cheeking buttercups, roly-poly kid in red footie pajamas on Christmas morning, flinging wrapping paper around the room. The two families are gathered once again at our parents' house. My daughter is a few years younger than my sister-in-law's first child. Shirley spends too much of the day monitoring her son, picking up, making sure he behaves and answers questions from the grandparents and does not eat too many Christmas cookies, which she has baked and set out. "One. You can have one," she tells the boy. "Not two." Leave him alone, I recall thinking; give him some space. If he eats a cookie too many, he'll upchuck, but she can't stop. It's like that sometimes with a first child. It's like that when a baby scares the daylights out of you with periodic breathing or central sleep apnea, and you think he's going to die.

I try a different tack, skirting advice. "Neuroscientists know about brain centers that stop individuals from doing certain things, inappropriate behaviors. They've identified parts of the frontal lobe, but if those areas are disrupted, maybe through injury or chemical intervention, then inhibitory connections can be shut down." I look at Shirley's adversarial lips.

"Why are you saying this, Ted?" She is about to unsnap her purse and dig but reconsiders, as if she has misplaced an accusatory tone. *This is your fault. You started it.* Maybe I did.

I shrug and continue. "Something called disinhibition. If the frontal lobe is dysfunctional, an individual sometimes can't stop himself from acting out in a certain way. From saying or doing something inappropriate, perhaps in a repetitive manner. A perseveration deficit, it's called."

She shakes the hair that reacts beautifully, thanks to a beauty product worth every penny. "He's better off in the Yaak, if that's where he is."

Fewer chances to run amuck, she means, claiming conviction falsely, for the fact is that in her every gesture and statement are mixed feelings. As in everyone.

"Might be true." I agree, though we do not know his whereabouts these days.

The toddler scampering through wrapping paper and allowed one sugar cookie grows up. He develops a personality. One day I see it: his Internet page, not so much through snooping as by chance. An investment client asks me to correspond through the social network, Facebook, which I have never had an interest in exploring. Never having viewed a single Facebook page, I nonetheless agree to the client's request and decide to give it a go. What can it hurt? I sign up and am instantly sent messages suggesting "friends," including younger family mem-

bers whose pages I scan as part of my experiment, thinking: what can it hurt? Not much, with trivia everywhere,
until I encounter my nephew's page and read what he has
written about the stupidity of federally funded programs
and the excellent NRA and idiot left-wing politicians.
Rather than a rainbow of suffering families in America,
he envisions a Black Sea of welfare recipients and foreigners churning the waters of corruption, fat and lazy
every one. His language is less poetic, racist, vulgar. Big
NRA supporter. Then I see the image he has posted. A
photograph. I call my brother who asks me what the devil am I doing looking at the kids's Facebook pages; what
business is it of mine? And maybe my brother has a point,
and possibly he has seen his son's photograph as well. My
brother remarks that Shirley looks online occasionally
too, but he doesn't admit to seeing the picture himself.
After a certain age, you stop monitoring the cookies.

Shirley is right, I believe, about a man who kills his
wife and kids out of the blue despite an instinct for sur-
vival. She is upset. She is ungrounded and has a right to
be. Or my example of a child terrified of free fall. Maybe
a million people consider shooting or jumping or slash-
ing every day or every hour for that matter – who knows
how often? For a thousand different reasons. Paranoia
or fried nerves or disinhibition. Crossed wires or drugs.
What are the chances a person will act out and do the un-
speakable sooner or later? Miniscule, taken individually.

I have been a pussycat to Shirley's panther up to now,

so I reverse rolls for a change and tell her. "You are right about the man who killed his family and then himself with a gun. The neighbors are right. His relatives are right. The shooter is right."

Shirley's glare would melt metal, yet a blink suggests some circuit of conscience sputters behind the baby blues as conduit to history and the fraying membrane of intentions.

"The *shooter* is right? A man who slaughters his wife and children is *right*? That's a grotesque thing to suggest! Just – "

My sister-in-law clutches her handbag as if preparing to sweep her pencil skirt and lovely locks out of my office. Instead, she cocks her head to something like the strains of Liszt's *Malediction* then stares at scarlet fingernails while thinking, I surmise, about her seven-bedroom, five-bathroom house on acreage kept immaculate year round for a son who will visit no more and a husband whose enthusiasm for her flesh – despite impeccable hair and gym-toned triceps and Retin-A treatments – diminished a decade ago, and knowing that the manicures and bedrooms and bathrooms and lawns and wiry limbs are indulgences – no, thin compensations – for hope and love gone sour. We are through the looking glass as I half-see, half-dream her – us – at a chic restaurant where she refuses to be seated by the staff because she must first wash her hair that is mis-styled into spit curls. She must do it now. At once. A restaurant where a customer can only be right, and a waiter asks me for our drink order. She pretends to massage and rinse as if this is the only place on earth to do so. In public, at a restaurant. Anywhere but at home, the unraveled property that is no home now. Father, brother, sister, mother not her relatives any more, nor husband nor children. She pauses at the threshold of a house that was her residence and wonders whether she can enter once more. Her life and the rumble of a sun failing to rise or the progress of a river gone dry, aromas of an empty kitchen and thoughts of caressing hands withdrawn.

My arm goes up, palm forward into a silent semaphore meaning: Let me explain.

★

On my nephew's Facebook page, following a tirade about progressive psychopaths and the entitlement society and violations of the Second Amendment is a photograph. It is a snapshot of Shirley's son, my nephew, holding a gun. The weapon is pointed into the camera lens. My nephew, my brother's son, Shirley's boy, the one who suffered from periodic breathing as an infant or central sleep apnea – not so much a "boy" now because he is about thirty years of age – and who is unmarried, unemployed, and angry, is aiming a gun at the lens, which is to say at the viewer. On his face is the shadow of something I interpret as subhuman tinted with equal parts satisfaction and metastasized rage, an emotional landscape without a sugar cookie in sight.

I am stunned by the photo and bring it to my brother's attention. He talks to Shirley. Parents respond first with denial but then confront their son. Dad and son argue. Son disappears into regions unknown, the Yaak, an acquaintance of my nephew suggests. We think it possible because he talked to his friends about such a place, though I need to Google the term to see where it is, what it means. Amusement park or insane asylum for fanatics? Likely both.

Shirley knows all this. She has lived it. She sees the headlines and is not innocent. She is intelligent and well read, though in my opinion inclined to self-indulgence. In my opinion because I am not a clinician or man of science, just an uncle and brother-in-law.

What she does not know is what she cannot know. She understands that the shooter in the newspaper committed a horrifying act. She's right. The neighbors and relatives are undoubtedly right in their expressed opinions that the shooter seemed to be the type of person who would never do such a thing. For all the neighbors know. For all the relatives know. The problem is that they are all right, and they are also wrong because the neighbor, the husband, the good father did such a thing. And a nation promoting free access to virtually any type of gun made it possible.

What does it feel like to be wrong when you don't know you are wrong? I keep asking myself this question. What is the inscape for a shooter who is so horrifyingly wrong yet does not know he is delusional or engaged in irreversible self-deception to the point of annihilation? It feels like being right. How does it feel when a person perceives life as hopeless and is convinced of that final truth? It feels like being one-hundred percent correct. I say some of these things to Shirley, not all.

What does it feel like to be that person's mother? To be Shirley, the parent, at this moment? Her fingers flutter as if they do not belong to anyone. Three framed photographs sit atop my desk. One of my wife and children, a second of my parents, taken during a wedding anniversary celebration when my dad was still in uniform. Shirley picks up the third picture and holds it inches from her face. It is the photo of her, my brother Gene, and their oldest son taken last Fourth of July. Shirley stands while extending the photograph in my direction and then slams the picture, glass-side down, on the top of my desk, shattering the glass. She almost totters off her stilettos, and I feel my hand going out, but only in imagination. She straightens, and the hair bounces back with every strand in place. She whispers through tears of a failed past catching up.

"You think he's damaged."

Psychologically she means, if firing electronic bullets is predictive of worse to come. But I am no soothsayer and cannot know that. What she really means is: *You think all this is my fault*, but I didn't say that.

What does it feel like to despise minorities or embrace them, to support or oppose abortion rights or women's rights or worker's rights or gay rights or any other political position? It feels right. To love guns? Right. To detest guns and everything they represent? Right again. To love and fear a son?

What are the chances of one person pulling a trigger, given the gene pool of a million people with as many urges and invented reasons bolstered with a perfect storm of alleles together with inhibition switched to the off position? Pick a number: say one in a million in a land of hundreds of millions. Spin the roulette wheel.

I think about what she has said and feel myself falling off the edge of a railing while Shirley, somewhere within herself, is poised eternally at the front door of her massive house, dark inside, wondering if she might enter and, if so, what she will find. The children gone off somewhere and echoes of a marriage; the odor of decaying expectation; dead calm rather than the commotion of a family with kids and parents rushing to keep up with life. Now only a faucet drips or window blind clicks somewhere down a hall; otherwise nothing today or tomorrow or next month, the house a maze of unlit chambers, dusty crevices, uninviting, cold, and – like Shirley – on standby for something to happen that might happen today or tomorrow or next month. Or never.

Her shoulders drop an inch as a tentacle of doubt twists her mouth. "He's better off there," Shirley repeats, meaning her cookie monster who used to tear through the living room in footie pajamas and now aims a high-powered weapon between the eyes of "friends" in cyberspace. Better off where people go feral. For now. Better there, as if we know where "there" is. Or maybe she means *we* are better off.

2. CLIFFORD, SOME YEARS AGO

Dumb to have messed up after being so careful. The fouled area might stay put if he paid attention and didn't touch anything else even though he wanted to test, was dying to see. How much he wanted to touch the spot with the other hand, yet must avoid touching, then wash his hands and get it off. Wash both hands several times before bedtime and during the night if he woke up but not using so much water that the rawness returned, making the skin crack and peel, as it had last week and the month before when his mom and dad turned purple-cheeked while shouting. So unfair to be restricted to a cup of water in the basin when all his brothers and sisters could refill the washbowl as much as they pleased without a peep from anyone or someone going after them around the house at the top of their lungs when they heard running water.

★

The boy, twelve years of age, appears to have no eyebrows or eyelashes until one looks closely and catches the sun shining, as it does now, on the oval face, hairs fine and golden, underlying skin taut as a violin string, shoulders reacting to a blast in the vicinity. But there has been no explosion.

Despite sunlight and a breeze sending ripples across waist-high grass, as if the Hand of God were waving forgiveness across the land, the last thing on the boy's mind this day is weather or The Almighty. It is the final week of summer vacation before school, the occasion reinforced by late-season insects abuzz. Only his hand, or more narrowly, the index finger of the left hand, occupies his thoughts however; how he must wash the finger and palm and then the other hand because it must contact the spot while washing. Touching it, spreading foulness so that the right hand must be scrubbed as thoroughly as the left, along with any other body part touching the left hand. To be safe. To be sure.

Pondering contamination with its cascade of associated possibilities, including condemnation, the boy makes his way to a silo poking skyward at the edge of the field of grass in which he finds himself, the only man-made structure for a quarter mile in any direction for a boy to investigate. A silo so ripe with abandonment, he notices upon drawing near, that an odor reminiscent of old age oozes through a cracked and rusted door at ground level. The smell seems to arise from something gone sickly sweet after death.

He approaches the silo door, yanks it with the good hand – the uncontaminated fingers – and enters, unmindful of wet silage penetrating shoes and then the seat of his trousers and beltline after he sits with his back against the curved wall. Contact with the odiferous foreign matter means nothing to him though, whatever else might be the matter.

Maybe I will never leave this place, he considers briefly, this silo in the middle of nowhere special, a quiet place where no one comes at you, yelling. A place that reminds you of a jungle plant rotting where it lived and died. Reminds you of a clock resisting advance, content. And of radios with their transmitters and receivers. A place that is. Just is. Safe.

His grandmother, he knows, thinks he might have been brain damaged somehow, way back, but no one else expresses an opinion about his head. Or his heart. Not out loud.

3. TED

One possibility to consider right from the get-go is that he might have been brain damaged. Might have been: as in, might not have been brain damaged, depending on who was expressing an opinion.

Young Ted first encountered the expression in a British movie, but the next week he overheard his aunt and uncle using the phrase while whispering about their son. Ted's straining ear caught the ambiguity.

"He's been at it again."

At it.

Ted thought they were poking fun at the language some British actors use in films, but the adults were not jesting. At it, as in their oldest boy, Clifford. As in over-enthusiastic manipulation, they meant, eagerness cranked up to compulsion. The parents, distressed more about ripple effects than morality, opined in a peevish duet that Clifford would go crazy if he kept at it. An agnostic version of: *Thou shalt not spill thy seed in vain*, to misquote Genesis 39:8-10. The directive was meant to warn three younger siblings against getting carried away when they attained the age of awakening. Clifford never went crazy, but he broadened his repertoire to hand washing with such vigor and frequency that fingers and palms went raw. Skin blistered and dissolved. Later in life he took to a wheelchair – always the boy had been awkward on his feet – and toward the end he would not stand at all, though his youthful wife and doctors believed him capable if he'd wanted to stand. They maintained there was nothing wrong with his legs or feet, other than flat arches, but he did not want to get up from the wheelchair any more, sound legs or otherwise, flat feet or no feet.

Something happened at a tender age that is suggestive. A week after he turned eight years old, Clifford invited Ted to his house on a Saturday morning along with four other schoolmates. Ted was born the same month as his cousin, and the two boys grew up within shouting distance, but they never bonded, so the invitation came as a surprise. Clifford herded the boys he considered to be neighborhood pals, including Ted, down into the basement to sit on folding chairs arranged in a semi-circle while he stood before them to talk about a club he wanted to start. The idea was to repair some simple radio transmitters and receivers – geeky skills at which he excelled – so that club members could hear special broadcasts. Clifford broadcasts. Clifford's ambition, which never came to much, was to become a radio personality, but the assembled boys already knew about that pipe dream from the annoying way he read aloud in school. Half way through an explanation of the club's objectives, Clifford's mother shouted something through the open door at the top of the stairs. When her language inclined to the disagreeable, the radio-personality-in-training grabbed a clothesline stretched below the ceiling, and he paced back and forth from one wall to the opposite while allowing the line to slide through his grip as angry sound waves from above ricocheted between his ears. He must have been wearing a ring because the cord returned a humming noise as he walked, the ritual evidently practiced as his breath quickened while his mother's voice boomed over the humming line. She stood somewhere in the shadows at the stair top, lobbing invectives at the boys –

"Your silly friends down there better... (blah)..."

– like so much soiled laundry –

"I told you before to get into your eff-ing room and clean up that... (blah, blah)..."

– while the pacing below continued, until one of the visiting boys rushed up the steps in the manner of an alarmed coyote and ducked out the back door, slamming it. Three other boys followed in a knot as Ted considered what to do. He knew this much: you don't turn on someone who is injured, or gnaw at a wound like an animal tasting blood. You don't abandon a relative in a difficult situation. You don't say no and walk away because it is indecent to do so. Even at eight years old, Ted knew. Yet Ted said no and walked away. Nothing more was mentioned about a radio project or boy's club with weekend meetings in the clothesline basement of Clifford's yellybeans house, but Ted's behavior that Saturday morning tugged at his conscience for months, years. Not Clifford's or his mother's, but Ted's. Something inside remained unsatisfied. Hungry. As time passed, decades, he felt more ravenous, but all that remained were a few crumbs of memory, and the feeling never went away. A hunger. But hunger for what?

Clifford's life, allotted a statistical mile, ended short of the mark by a few thousand feet. Why? It is possible to seek answers to the wrong questions or invoke cause and effect where no such relation is in play. It is possible, Ted understood, to ask pointless questions that lead nowhere and take seriously suggestions devoid of merit.

At the funeral, one of the grandparents hinted Clifford's brain might have been slightly damaged from the start. Why slightly, and how did it happen? Or not happen? This much we know because this is what we are told. God lives in all things and has a home base somewhere beyond the clouds. He is an all-knowing father who is capable of splendid works and apparent whimsy and terrible wrath for reasons not always clear to mortals. It is not obvious, for example, why Clifford died decades before the age predicted in actuarial tables maintained by insurance companies. It is also said that the devil skulks underground where it is hot and smelly, probably from sulfur fumes or putrescine or something unimaginably worse. A mortal cannot imagine the stench because a fallen human must die and enter Hades to find out. The ancient Greeks thought the gate to Hades was located at the southern tip of the Peloponnese, but that idea has grown out of favor over the centuries. Satan's job is temptation, but what he's really after – we are told – is the big paycheck, a person's soul. No one knows whether God or the devil harvested Clifford's, but some people think "fiddling with yourself" privately puts a black mark on a person's soul. Or eating meat on Good Friday. Or maybe not if a person's thinking equipment is damaged or he is of some "other faith" that shoves wrong ideas into his head, in which case the unenlightened person is or is not culpable in the eyes of his maker. We just don't know the details.

Paradoxes abound when it comes to Clifford and family opinions on the topic of that particular, peculiar family member. It's a problem for Ted in several ways. Number one: he does not like to be left hanging when it comes to family issues. Number two: Ted now has two boys in their teens. He would like to relate the Clifford incident as a cautionary tale but knows that parents should not preach to offspring. Many experts insist this is true – about preaching – and they have been preaching that advice for years. Number three: another paradox – or brainteaser if you prefer the term – is that if parents do not take the lead in guiding the next generation (and, yes, preaching if it comes to that) then who will?

Politicians perhaps. Officeholders are elected to solve problems, but it is widely held that they are no good at much other than raising campaign contributions. Pedophile priests – a paradox in and of itself, requiring no predicate (but here is one anyway) – cannot always be trusted. Perhaps mathematicians can help out with paradoxes and enigmas because math is the discipline, brainy folks assert, that comes closest to what human beings can comprehend about truth or certainty in our universe. (We say "our universe," meaning absolutely everything but hinting there might be more than one universe, yet another paradox or semantic pleonasm at the very least.) Insurance companies rely on math and statistical records to generate predictions about life events, including the age at which a male like Clifford might be expected to die, slight brain damage or none. Math gives us concepts such as infinity and irrational numbers and the idea that there is no greatest cardinal number. Statistical predictions are expressed in terms of mathematical probability with all its formulaic baggage. These disciplines create more difficulties for understanding, so the fields of so-called truth along with their probability and truth tables are mixed blessings for all but a few souls possessed of exceptional tolerance for vagueness, black marks or not – from eating meat or horsing around with themselves – on their incorporeal essence.

Enough. This is all too confusing. What Ted wants is a roadmap for living and learning and getting along and dying, something tangible to reveal what really is or is not up with family members and others he cares about. It is doubtful that the question of eating meat on Good Friday or any other day would be resolved to everybody's satisfaction even with a roadmap, but other issues might be rendered a bit less foggy.

So Ted worked up a roadmap, admittedly a rough draft. If he can summon the courage to complete it and show it to his boys one day, he will explain that the roadmap is designed to be read across each row from left to right. Given the nature of adolescents and possibility of free will, they can also read backwards or down or up the columns. Ditto if free will is a myth. He will also advise his boys to relax while looking around: the roadmap isn't lengthy, and there is no exam, but it just might contain a useful suggestion or two about family matters and life in general. Here is what Ted has fashioned so far.

Truth and Wisdom	Lies and Ignorance
I think, therefore I am	Anyone claiming to know the truth
Know thyself	Anyone claiming to know thyself
Mahatma Gandhi	Virtually all other politicians, living or dead, but see #1, above
The world as we perceive it is rarely the world as it is	The world as we perceive it
2 + 2 equals 4 always, everywhere	Treating unequals equally
God and the imagination are one	God made me do it
DNA and your environment	Free will, fate
First, do no harm	War to end wars
Genuine art (you know it when you see it)	Bad art (critics can tell you what that is*)
Doubt (if scientific)	Doubt (if religious)
Faith (if religious)	Faith (if scientific)
Good questions	There are no bad questions*
The simplest explanation is the best	Ghosts, monsters, UFOs, astrology
The Internet	The Internet
Moby Dick, the book	Hollywood film versions of great literature, except for To Kill A Mockingbird
Public radio and TV on a good day	Commercial radio and TV, especially FOX if you are a Democrat or MSNBC if Republican
Compassion	Judging the universe

*Not really. Remember, this is the "Lies and Ignorance" column.

Ted, fully grown now and trying to manage a family of his own, is aware that the roadmap is still rough around the edges. He would be the first to encourage his two boys, or anyone else, to move entries around from one side of the table to the other and challenge the statements. He does not want to insult anyone, and he would also want everyone to know that some of the ideas are not his, but come from people who smart people call smart: Socrates, Aristotle, Descartes, and William of Occam way back in history, or the Dalai Lama more recently. Ted is simply trying to get things right in his mind, and if he has to borrow ideas, so be it. One reason for Ted's struggle is that his immediate family and other relatives, living and dead, keep bumping into his life, and not always in a pleasant way. The more he reflects on the Clifford business for instance, the more he realizes he does not know, rather like string theory, and this realization does not lend confidence when trying to figure out the right thing to think about the past or do in the present.

Is Ted coping better now that he has a preliminary roadmap? Is he less hungry? A few more details about the relatives are instructive at this juncture. Where to start?

Here. There are only four people still alive these days who might have the genuine lowdown on Clifford. The "truth" so to speak. Ted's Aunt Sarah (Clifford's mom) remains locked in a two-note song of her own making, which alternates between episodes of mumbling depression and bouts of yelling, whether anyone is around to hear or not. Ted's Uncle Sid (Clifford's dad) slid into madness in late mid-life after killing someone – or nearly killing someone or possibly a couple of people. Rumors continue to circulate among family members that somebody dropped baby Clifford on his head a week after he was born, or his brain was slightly deprived of oxygen during a difficult birth, or he nearly drowned in some bathwater, all of which could shed light – or maybe not – on the way the firstborn son lived and died, if the details were ever verified, but asking either of Clifford's parents at this point is a pointless exercise.

Who else might have some information? Ted has a brother who is doing okay, and his brother has a son who is not doing okay. The son loves guns, really loves guns. The son is so messed up that it worries the entire family, and Ted would never dream of adding to this brother's troubles by bringing up his own. Ted's wife entered the picture too late and knows virtually nothing about Clifford. Ditto Ted's two teenage boys. Ted's oldest daughter is struggling to become a successful artist in the Big Apple. She has met with marginal success in the competitive art scene and has been trying to work out relationship kinks with a hunky carpenter – "kinks" and "hunky" are her poetic descriptors – an affiliation rather more physical than emotionally satisfying, if a parent is to read between the relationship lines; therefore, this daughter is of some concern to her parents, but she never met Clifford.

Ted's parents are still living independently in their

platinum years, and they could probably offer some real insight; however, two difficulties render a conversation about Clifford unlikely. First, it's a strain when they come to visit for the holidays or during summer because the elders are disinclined to specify an end date for a stay-over at Ted's sprawling suburban house. They see no need to set a departure date "because we're family," and the length-of-stay disinclination causes visits to begin and end in hurt feelings more often than not. Tensions run high with the parents. Second, both parents seem to be developing Alzheimer's disease, and it is difficult to know what to believe or not believe when talking to them about anything.

"What time would you like to have dinner, Dad?"

"This is a funny time to be having breakfast."

"Let's plan on six o'clock."

"Won't we be gone by then?"

Verdict out then as to the reason a boy might be slower than most on his feet, odd in his thinking, wacky in his behavior, wavy handed when trying to catch a ball. It was his parents' fault; no one is to blame; it is not about blame at all. Spin of the roulette wheel with winners and losers, but is it fair to ask questions about way-back-when, advisable to go poking around for guilty parties, or helpful to probe when there might be no satisfying resolution to decades-old family secrets about Clifford?

Ted is worried about more than a prematurely deceased cousin, to wit, his finances, his health, his oldest daughter because he wants her to be happy, his nephew because the young man might be dangerous to himself or others, people who drop out of school at a young age, the unemployed and unemployable, the paradox of murder to rid the world of murderers, the likelihood that his parents are developing dementia, animal abuse, how he will pay for the younger kids' college educations, and the usual things about which he might have some, or absolutely no, control. Ted seems unable to stop revisiting the Clifford experience and wondering what he might have done differently.

Driving his cushy Mercedes to the office this morning, thirty or forty-some years on, Ted feels it in his chest again, a nail through the heart. He wishes he could bundle up events ruining that ugly basement day like so much dirty underwear and toss them into a washer then hang the stuff on a line to dry in the sunshine. Or that a track coach had been around to blow the whistle when it mattered. Someone calling a false start. Making everyone pull up, march right back to toe the line, and start over again. But no: there is no high-efficiency scrubber for memories, no retroactive coach or timeouts.

Instead, Ted has settled on a working hypothesis. Thinking is a good thing, he thinks, a necessary and human thing, but as with his cousin's behavior, a person can take a thing too far and end up with anatomical or spiritual chaffing from overuse. As far as roadmaps are concerned, several are already out there for people who want one – for some it's the Bible or Second Amendment or Golden Rule; for others it's the scientific method or Charles Darwin – but instead of getting bogged down with roadmaps suggesting what is philosophically right and wrong, what is truth or falsehood, Ted is beginning to see the importance of behavior over thought, the idea that it's not what people think about something that's critical but what they do.

The thing wanted is not tolerance or a sense of decency so much as real behavior that makes a difference. What is needed for a troubled child is action.

Translation: the boys downstairs that awful day could have traced conspiratorial circles in air at their temples, as kids do, and whispered *"Grown ups!"* as they giggled about a batty mother's intrusion, but eight-year-olds are short on perspective. It is difficult enough to know how to respond to a fuming adult who takes you by surprise, entirely another thing for a child to live with such a person.

The recollection of visiting Clifford's house while growing up reminds Ted of walking in tall grass. Most of the time everything is fine and dandy during a jaunt, but once in a while you come home with a tick under the skin, or almost step on a snake. Clifford was a tick with a tic, a disturbing bugger and annoying as all get out, but hardly dangerous; at least one adult in his world resembled a poisonous serpent lying in wait, and you never knew if the creature was dozing or poised to spring.

These days Ted thinks about a Saturday morning when he was eight-years-old. He remembers a singing clothesline and cascade of angry words going in one ear and failing to come out the other. He concludes there is one idea favored above others by the various religions. You name it. Judaism. Islam. Christianity. One word echoed in philosophy through the centuries and spoken repeatedly these days by the Dali Lama. One concept on the roadmap that feels right all the time. Compassion. Ted thinks that compassion would have lightened the load at least for a few hours while Clifford was alive.

Indeed, he might have returned to that wretched basement with its humming clothesline to tinker with a radio shoulder-to-shoulder with his tick-tic of a cousin, or invited the boy over to his own house for some peace and quiet away from the serpent. Not just feeling something, but an act of compassion might have been the ticket – but Ted would never say that aloud even now because he dislikes know-it-alls. Wouldn't say it to his wife, Lavinia, or to his two sons or older daughter. Ted is a lousy advocate because he, like most folks, has a poor track record when it comes to doing the right thing at the proper moment.

4. UNCLE SID

I am writing my Congressman for the first time because he needs to understand the most important thing in my life. It's not money or sex. With all due respect, he can keep his kickbacks and Italian cars and fast women. I only need my arms, but first a person needs to define his terms. That's where history helps.

When the Indians told Lewis and Clark to watch out for bears (native people didn't know they are called grizzlies like we know today), the explorers snickered and killed their first griz with one shot. Thump on the ground. "What's all the hoopla?" they winked, seeing no problem with killing a big bear because President Jefferson gave them the right to bear arms, and they took their bear arms wherever they went. Good thing because a worse grizzly came along one day and kept coming at them despite several shots until somebody had to jump off a cliff to get away. True story. They kept shooting until they got their bear, but without the right to bear arms how could they wipe out the bears, or how could troops kill all the Indians during the uprisings? Every pioneer would be dead. So that's what arms are, whatever works in a situation to defend yourself and put things right. If a handgun works, that's a person's arms. If an

Uzi is needed, so be it, or my AK47.

Some people want to draw an artificial line. For arms control I say go ahead and limit those nuclear weapons in the Mideast and Africa because fanatics live there, but I'm a citizen of the United States of America, which God has blessed, and I can have my arms because Amendment 2 says. Now in a crowded movie or building where a maniac starts shooting innocent people, naturally a bomb won't work, but if everybody has guns then maybe a dozen people shoot back. Goodbye shooter. Same thing for schools or street situations where everybody standing around shoots the shooter. Can't miss. That's how it works in the Constitution because our forefathers understood today's reality.

Goons traipsing around today are robbing people blind. Someone sees an illegal criminal with an automatic hiding under a hoodie, and he's got a situation and maybe he needs to shoot the guy period. How else does a man protect his family? Any analyst will tell you. I've talked to them.

Folks gripe how more people are killed in this country than in all the wars. Count the deaths from the Revolution and Civil War, World War I and II, and Vietnam and all, and it's twice the number killed at home by guns than over there in wars, but here's the question: Is that a bad thing? Take those punks shooting each other in the big cities. Or those dead foreigners. Where would they be if they weren't dead? In prison mostly, and that's a fact.

How much does it cost to keep them in prison? Twice as much as putting them in college. So bang, they shoot each other on the street and taxpayers don't shell out for prison and can send their kids to college.

Here's another argument nobody can deny. Guns are popular for old people when things get bad. Look it up. I have a friend whose dad is 92-years-old. The old guy still reads a newspaper with his oatmeal, only now the morning paper is upside-down on the table. Dementia, so my friend had to put him in a home. After a year, he figured how much it cost the old man. Hospice nursing came to $120K, the residential home another $48K, medical bills $30K, and he needed radiation to boot. The total comes to $200K every single year. Put the cash in one hand and a bullet in the other, and the choice is a no brainer. Bam. Money in the bank. Take his guns and he's a criminal for using one, or he's $200K in debt for not. No sir, I don't think so.

Teddy Roosevelt didn't trust people who did not hunt. He was the President, and he wasn't talking bows and arrows. In the olden days there weren't any supermarkets with lunchmeat, so how do you think they got their sandwiches? When I was six, my uncle put a .22 semi-automatic rifle in my hands and said squeeze the trigger. Don't jerk. The recoil knocked me back, but I almost got a squirrel. Now I love shooting but I learned squeezing my gun beats jerking it any day. I have thought long and hard about being like any other red-blooded American man engorged with certain unalienable endowments, but I can't always show it in public. What I can do is kill something with wings or claws like before with passenger pigeons for target practice, or now with buffaloes to mount their heads on a wall to show people. Did not our Maker create superior creatures to reign over inferior, predator over prey? What good is a buffalo on the prairie chewing grass meant for cows and pigs? Take away the right of one of God's creatures and you strip a man of his manliness. Natural selection I say; live and let live.

It's never been proven when you take away guns that gun violence goes down other than in airports and courtrooms or prison or hospitals that don't have guns. Science says you can't prove a negative. If arms are outlawed, only outlaws will have arms, then how can troubled teens who like guns channel themselves? How can law-abiding citizens hunt and shoot them – illegal punks and fence-jumping aliens I mean, or psychos on a rampage? Don't make me an outlaw.

It's not like NRA people are making a killing with more guns. They are foot soldiers protecting Amendment 2 for every honest citizen with inbred rights to buy another gun to kill a terrorist or buffalo or overthrow the government, whatever is needed. Trust a patriot to recognize his natural endowments and how to defeat lame opinions out there. Guaranteed.

5. TED AND HIS NEPHEW

He didn't have a page of his own, indeed had never seen one. The whole business was designed for the under-thirty crowd and much younger, Ted imagined, until the afternoon a prominent client requested that unexpected form of networking. Prospects of a windfall for little effort sent a prickle down his spine. Surely nothing would be lost by giving it a try.

He entered his name and e-mail address, chose a password, identified his birthdate and gender. Simple as that. A click sent him across the Rubicon to dock at the most bustling social port in history then off the gangplank for a plunge into electronic quicksand.

Thumbnail photos of "People you may know" instantly populating the monitor sucked him in for a closer inspection of acquaintances he had not thought about in years. Him? Her? Yes, Ted did know them. Pals from junior high and college along with an ex-sister-in-law. The familiar faces of two nephews and their much younger sister, Pebbles.

Start with Pebbles. Ted opted to "friend" his niece for a trial run he thought could do no harm until a gerbil raced across the screen. *Meriones unguiculatus*. Was that normal or a network hiccup? He flashed on the Richard

Gere legend about a gerbil extracted from whence one ought not be then scanned Pebbles' page with its feature shot of a nine-year-old with iPhone held to a mirror. Posters of Britney Spears and K-Pop stars taped on a bedroom wall in the background. Recent entries about gerbils and drawings of little pink ponies. She wished for a pony on a star that made iffy magic possible. Older posts all of a kind.

Mom burned spaghetti for lunch. Going to get a glue gun. (Smiley face.)

Who's the smartest one in class and why am I? Heehee

My cousin bought an ugly scarf at Target. LOL (Frowny face.)

Recurrent gushings about boyfriends this and girlfriends that and her kingdom for a blanket reproducing the Confederate flag. Really? Did she understand its unhappy symbolism or just like the design? Naïve, but best to leave advice on the topic to her parents. Yes, really, Facebook was for kids: confirmation at hand as Ted closed the Pebble page.

From a gallery of other names, he spotted a Larkspur. Good old Didi Larkspur from sixth grade. Oh, and a date with her after one varsity basketball game if memory served, just the one date in senior high. OK. Give it a try, friend.

A click returned a snapshot of double-chinned Didi splayed in a rocker, semi-frontal view of the very-today Ms. Larkspur stroking a lap cat, corpulent strokee and stroker both underemployed and ruttish looking. Odds favoring garlicky household and cat box aromas. He ventured downstream to survey scenes from Didi-Land as if catapulting straight into her garden after decades of disassociation.

Inspection of her produce revealed low-hanging blossoms ripening into interrogatives. *Are you reimagined, sinner? Are you washed in the blood of the Lamb?*

No, and lord no. A modern woman might believe what she would, but still...

A stroll down the path of interrogatives sent Ted stumbling into the vegetable bin of Didi's noggin with its holy of holies, bringer of rapture, and high priest of zucchinis for, indeed, it – or he or she or whatever – did look like a giant zucchini.

Z-O-N-I-N-E!

Have you joined Zonine? a caption beneath the image asked of the viewer.

Zonine, shepherd and overlord, Didi advised her flock of social media followers, was from a dimension beyond one's piddling planetary purview. Beyond time and the Milky Way. Beyond the beyond.

And beyond all reason, Ted decided. She must be joking, this schoolmate he'd once thought clever and svelte. Zone 9 from outer space? A gag, surely.

Or maybe not. Ted waved a search-engine wand to banish overlords from further consideration, Googling "blood of the Lamb" for redirection. The Princeton.edu website clarified. "To be washed in the blood of the Lamb is to be washed by virtue of the blood of Jesus, that is, by virtue of His death." He closed the Princeton page and re-entered the nest of Zonine's Venus for a final gander. There lurking in a monstrous rendering of a bad day at Calvary, blood trickling from blackened orbits shadowed under a tangle of cruel prickers beneath a crown of furry clouds on the verge, he found the suggestion – the merest hint mind you – of a UFO-like vessel floating in the bramble haze.

Enough. Best to exit the thicket, but how? Connect on the Internet after decades of silence then disconnect? Or in the verbifying language of the medium, to friend and instantly "unfriend" Didi? Without question an insult, but was it not an insult to oneself to remain connected?

Decide later. He bid adieu to Didi and conjured his nephew.

Directly below the photograph of a clean-shaven, mid-thirties fellow came a rant favoring the National Rifle Association and castigating detractors as "... you bunch a stupid idiots." Malefic language accompanied more pleonasms leading to a big thumbs-up for concealed carry. No brainer to require schoolteachers to strap on holsters and stock classrooms with assault weapons, his nephew believed. Generalizations about Amendment 2 and political erosion of mankind and heaven itself, or something. Pep talk on bullets for all, garnering a dozen "likes."

Ted blew a silent Ooo into air while scooting his chair away from the screen. Functional brain tissue might be in short supply everywhere – by definition half the 7+ billion biped-capable (minus one dead center on the bell curve) had an IQ less than 100 – but his own flesh and blood? Ted extended fingers to the keyboard again, typing rapidly.

Do you really believe what you are suggesting? I am disappointed. More: ashamed. Who are you anyway? Your Uncle Ted.

He hit the return key. Comment posted.

Instant regret assailed his conscience as a flight of electronic pigeons charged the cloud to alight in user-friendly in-boxes across a wired nation. One thoughtless twitch and he'd violated his own rule about courtesy. Never get low and scratch the dirt. Write something then wait. Temper the tone after the fire abates. Revise, then don't ship it or post it. Don't say it or e-mail it, especially not to a family member. Assuredly not to a nephew of an age too advanced for tantrums but too immature for political perspective. But how to deal with those online expressions of wrath, the lashings out in us-versus-them cyberspace? And for what purpose had his nephew written them? For attention? From whom? Doubtless his gun-happy relative had become a bullhorn for the NRA with the bluster amplified through a cone of pathetic and appalling self-interest, but now this. A personal failure of restraint. An uncle, guilty as the nephew.

Ted ran up to the roof deck for a shot of air to clear the head. Nighttime. The Pleiades rising and a sense of objects floating in space. Vagabond musings of extending one's reach into the void and grasping the floaters to shepherd them safely home à la Zonine. Imagined control having nothing to do with reality.

Ted scrambled back inside and down the stairs to the home office again. Those four walls. The ceiling and floor closing in to grind the brain to porridge. Image of the social network as a cosmos shrinker assessable to all at light speed with the tap of a digit. Enticing people to fume and fiddle.

He's a redneck. She's a wacko. You don't always want to know, Ted mused, but once you do know, there's no going back.

Surely, he was mistaken about what he'd read. Returning to the monitor, he scrutinized several of his young relative's comments in search of the man whose boyish hand had once shot out to clutch an uncle's in trust, or if not the man, the adult, then an explanation for what the boy had become. To discover a trace of common sense behind harangues in all caps, rude code for Internet screaming. To uncover logic despite bursts of grammatical and spelling errors, testament to the sorry state of education across the land. To hunt for rationality among volleys of explodents endorsed by chorus lines of exclamation points. But in lieu of reason or a boy or the man, Ted found blasts aimed at fat welfare moms. Poison for nappy-haired tricksters pimping the system. Mocking photographs of "dikes" and "fagits." Verbal grenades hurled at straw-man targets born on foreign soil. Then one last image caused Ted to stop mid-scroll and stare at the monitor. A photograph of his nephew, maniacal eyeballs glaring, with a gun pointed into the camera lens. The kind of image about which people ask questions painful and obvious after the fact. Why didn't anyone speak up? Why didn't someone do something?

In longhand on a sheet of noncommittal paper, and seated as far from electronic gadgetry as he could manage within the office, he jotted notes in ink, calming and safe. Focus on one thing, Ted counseled himself. Start small with a first draft to set aside and reconsider.

Next day he revised his arguments. That evening, he reworked the revision.

My Dear Nephew,

I scanned your Facebook page the other day, pausing at comments about welfare recipients among other topics. Statistics can be cited to support any viewpoint, but here are data from three sources that agree on the numbers. They originate from the Center on Budget and Policy Priorities, The Washington Post, *and* National Review.

91% of all Federal "entitlement dollars" go to the el-

*derly, disabled, and working households. Less than 3%
of the population is on welfare. The wealthiest 20% of
households receive two-thirds of Federal tax dollar ex-
penditures.*

*When I see you next December over the holidays, let
us share a libation and sing Christmas carols as you polish
your smoking gun, avoiding our definitions of what con-
stitutes compassion and welfare. Of who is "them" and
who is "us." Of the possibility that "they" are us. Of
the likelihood that people outside your center are a center
too. Of the truths that when one sees people, one tends to
converse; when one sees demons, one demonizes. It seems
impossible, I know, but some people are having a worse
day than you.*

Ted tossed under the covers that night a salad of mixed
dreams populated by wee horses and fat cats. A side dish
of glue guns, dreamy crooners, and bloody prickers. A
feast for machine-gun-armed teachers hither and spirit
guides yonder and Stagger Lees all around. He wakened
to modulations of Bruckner's roller coaster Ninth Sym-
phony from the clock radio and reread his own composition before completing a Microsoft Word document.
Abdominal protestation rippled his insides as he fluttered
over the keyboard wondering why. Why so troubled?
Was he as out of touch as his brother's son? Would any
response, no matter the care taken or caring expressed,
only feed the visceral flames? His nephew had gone crude

and substandard, but what was the right thing to do at this point?

A ringing phone interrupted his soliloquy. His brother, Gene, on the line.

"What are you doing?"

"Having coffee."

"No. What are you doing on Facebook?"

"Work. A client requested I correspond that way."

"You know Facebook is for kids, don't you?" Gene's voice cracked.

"So I thought, but I see your wife has a page."

"Shirley wants to keep tabs on the kids. That's all."

"What's on your mind?"

"Your nephew. What are you thinking?"

Best to proceed carefully. "I read some of his posts. Have you seen them?"

A pause at the other end. "Shirley tells me about them occasionally. So now you send him a comment? Why on earth would you do that, Ted?"

"Shock, I suppose. My own."

"Don't read what he writes then."

"That's the answer?"

"You're not going to change his mind."

"I wasn't trying to change his mind."

"What then?"

"Maybe to get him to think before he writes."

"Good luck with that."

"It's as much about me as him. I find his remarks disturbing. Have you seen the photo of him pointing a gun at the camera?"

No answer from Gene.

"Anyway, I drafted something. I'm considering sending it to your son. Not on Facebook of course, but directly to him by e-mail. I'd like you and Shirley to read it first."

"Sure. Send it to us."

Ted did so and within the hour received an e-mail reply from Shirley and a phone call from his brother, both unequivocal. Don't send it. Ever. Don't do anything unless jeopardizing an uncle's relationship with a nephew was the objective. Predictable parental responses for maintaining the status quo: hope for the best, harmony on the horizon, that kind of thing. Desire centered on denial until the other shoe dropped.

His brother called the next morning to say he had talked with his son over the phone. Rather, they had screamed accusations back and forth.

"You did the very thing you told me not to do, Gene."

"I know. I did. He's my son."

"So how did you leave it?"

"Not good.

A couple days later the son knocked on the door of his parent's house and remained standing on the stoop. He wouldn't come in. He wouldn't leave. He seemed unable or unwilling to speak. He took the glasses from his father's face – the ones for computer reading – and dropped them on the stoop to grind them into the cement.

Then a follow-up phone exchange between the brothers.

Ted cleared his throat. "Can I do anything to help?"

"Please." Obvious irony in his brother's voice.

Things mellowed by December. The nephew chuckled an apology and bought his dad a new pair of glasses. At Christmas he gave his sister Pebbles a gerbil and admitted he sometimes sat up too late at night in a rage to vent on the computer. Shouldn't do it, he supposed. He gave every appearance of coming to terms with his betters save for telltale signs a watchful Ted encoded. The nephew nodded too much, seemed agreeable to everything, and said "absolutely" too many times after someone made a statement. Absolutely. Absolutely, as if he were not listening at all, as if he might be treading indifferent water in a tiny and unswimmable pool.

The water-treader did not bear up for long. After the holidays the sinking man let his hair drift and beard flow. He allowed his body to baste itself in natural juices. Swapped hygiene for God-given ripeness. On his collar grew tiny clusters of eggs akin to transparent grapelets, but as he overlooked the personal vermin others noted on his skin, so he ignored the hatchlings crawling between sheets and mattress in the small hours.

In spirit he vanished, then in fact, according to a college buddy, into the Yaak. He'd been heard praising a haven where cell phones don't roam but wolverines and antelope play in extreme northwest Montana. A vast and frigid remoteness where seldom is heard an encouraging word because the scattered retirees and homeschoolers keep their distance from one another while socially exfoliated survivalists, though reportedly housebroken, aren't interested in chatting with anyone about anything. Leave'em alone there to do as they will, and they'll leave you alone too. Probably.

Unserviced by phone or power lines, the nephew's Facebook page together with his expressed views went quiescent, and the rest was silence except for lamentation from a space once occupied by a boy's extended hand. Attempts by Ted and his brother Gene to reconnect with the young man failed. Return to sender. Address unknown.

Playbook for tots to wish upon a star and family album for the sincere, Ted reflected late one night. Scrapbook for the self-righteous and soapbox for the delusional. Facebook is merely a tool, he decided. Don't blame the tool. A way to connect and disconnect; gateway drug and carnival cruise for a trip from not knowing to knowing. And back again from knowing to not knowing or wanting to know.

6. TED'S PARENTS

From her machine-gun mouth spewing radioactive ammo at 8 a.m. on Sunday, she delivers the line along with eggs and potatoes seasoned, he imagines, with oregano. "I don't love you." No herbal dusting, but mounds of oregano to upset a queasy stomach.

So begins the morning, the hour, of jockeying when he must confront the question that spurs neural nets to electrochemical overdrive. Which beat, the neurons demand. I... don't... love... you. Four words spoken with no malice he can detect in response to anything said this day; indeed, he has yet to open his mouth for eggs or potatoes or repartee. Not in ages has a declaration – this one riding the heels of a tirade about a neighbor or some other vexation – so fluttered his butterflies and scrambled brainwaves. What is the meaning of the *non sequitur*, peculiar for its monotone delivery as if she were remarking absently about poppies blooming on a backyard slope visible through their picture windows, and how is he to respond?

Countermeasures hinge on the beat, so he tries to reconstruct her intonation but finds himself wondering how long it's been since he's paid much attention to anything she says. The new thermostat. That's how long.

Weary of squabbling about discomfort in the house – too chilly for her of a morning downstairs, too warm upstairs at bedtime – he consults a heating expert who recommends a programmable unit. Never mind the hassle of installing a separate regulator and damper in his study so at least one zone can be controlled in a rational manner; never mind the expense to achieve harmony.

"It's no good." Her reaction. "You tinker with the thing!"

Such bunk. Tartuffery. He does not tinker but programs the master unit for high-tech functions and withdraws. Having none of it, she dashes to the hardware store and returns with the insulting purchase, brandishes a screwdriver and mounts (ineptly) a plastic cover on the wall. A lock box to secure the new thermostat, one with the single key tucked always in her pocket. "To keep the grandkids from fidgeting with the thing." Only one key supplied, she maintains. Certainly, dear.

I don't love you, accent on the initial beat, is the first interpretation to rankle his synapses. Of alternative readings, each augmented by guilt, this is the trickiest because it suggests that someone certainly *does* love him – someone other than his wife – the good woman is aware of the fact, and she might know the paramour. Lola of course, for what is life without a smidgen of adultery? Shameless, elegant Lola whom he had canoodled for two years when unknowing spouses absented themselves for shopping expeditions or flights afield. Which was often enough to enjoy warmth – salty sex, but was it love? – without the burden of conjugal pressure until Lola breaks it off after a friend of hers confides over another round of martinis that a woman must be vigilant in a hamlet where even the woodwork has eyes and ears. That guilty parties must be wary of duped spouses who may be less unknowing than schemers think. The affair ends: how many months ago? Three. Four? But is it over – not over?

Wary, even paranoid, of the very woodwork. Like the manufacturer's label on the underside of the wooden seat flipped up and conscientiously down again after countless harangues about failing to leave the seat down – Bevis the label might be, or Bemis, something like that. One looks but does not always see; hears but does not listen. She, the most verbose woman he has ever known, fuming around the clock about the state of the commode or crumbs on a newly scrubbed floor when it is the house-keeper who sanitizes every household surface rather than she. As if it were the male's responsibility to monitor the seat each time after tinkling, rather than a matter of in-difference for two adults who frequent the shared facility equally. The lid. Another of his failures. Another of her tricks. Down rather than up for her convenience; never mind his own.

Trickery. As if he does not understand the chicanery to which his better half resorts. After years of tongue-lash-ing, he has taught himself to remember: do your business then pivot the seat down. Never up but down, always down. How he leaves it, dutifully, and still she storms, still she comes at him with passion in her voice. "You left it up again after I told you! What's wrong with you? Have you no brain in that head anymore?" Until he begins to question his memory, fret about Dr. Alzheimer at this point in life. Could it be true? Has he blanked again and left the seat up? Until he witnesses the shocking behavior with his own eyes after finishing up and darting into the pantry across the hall – waiting with the door ajar – to watch his wife enter the spare bathroom on the main floor and lift the seat up (up!) then exit while shouting his name to complain about the attitude of the commode. Or had he dreamed the scene? Or mis-remembered it?

I *don't* love you. The second beat. As if he presumed to correct her by declaring that she absolutely must love him, when he has made no such statement since nuptials. He cannot discount this option, though it is less likely than the first, because it is perfectly in character for her to chastise him for something he has not said or done. Not thought or felt. Something not true. Like his enjoyment of "that racket," as she calls it. Racket. Mahler, the most inspired and forward-thinking composer of Romantic-era masterworks for classical orchestra. Among the greatest composers of all time, per Lenny Bernstein who knew a little something about music. No Mahler? Well then, try something different for a change, my pet. Sample the post-modern equivalent of two-step euphony. Lend an ear to the latest generation of dance and alternative music pulsing through contemporary airwaves. Hearken as we test the limits of six new speakers plus subwoofer to replicate in Dolby© Digital Plus E-AC-3 advanced 7.1 surround sound the rhythmic thump, thump, thumping of energized electronic music designed to rocket twenty-somethings into sweaty raptures in clubs and rave warehouses across the Western hemisphere. Post-punk and trans-hardcore fusion electronica. He finds he likes it. Enjoys the pounding all the more at a volume inducing hearing loss. So delicious when she yells something but cannot hear herself over the thump, thump, thumping from the subwoofer. "Turn that god-awful noise off!" Or words to that effect. Thump, thump, thump. "It's making you deaf!" But of course he cannot hear her, will not hear. Thump, thump, thump. Lid up. Seat down. Thermostat on, off, on again. But he cannot see as well as before and knows not to look in her direction.

He visualizes her words as weapons stockpiled in a drawer of knives and other treacherous implements. Or no, as the knives themselves, a vocabulary of accessible cutlery clinging to the magnetized wall holder and scattered about countertops, for her father, rest his soul, had been a butcher who collected knives, then a grocery owner before developing a profitable franchise. His daughter the inheritrix of shiny, dangerous blades always available for a purpose, catching the sun, each designed for a job — slicing, mincing — like her words. Knives bequeathed by Daddy and within her reach. For him to reach as well if he decides to hold one to assess its weight in the hand or test a blade-sharp edge against the skin, for a knife is control, authority. A knife is handy to wield, as one will, to slash if one is bold or thrust or throw. But she is moving again, scurrying across the Carrara marble she requires on a kitchen floor – because nothing else will do – to extract items and deposit others in the double-wide refrigerator – nothing else will serve – as she continues to chatter about god-knows what.

Not today then, but tomorrow perhaps, he can shovel deep into the loam of the backyard slope and when enough earth is excavated invite her to see. To inspect his new "vegetable patch." Or if she were to refuse, then force her at knifepoint with one of her daddy's fine blades, march her out back to inspect his excellent labor by peering down, down into the pit where a rotting carcass might after a cycle of seasons supplement the soil with nitrogen and potassium and trace minerals. Then, when microbes and earthworms have done their duty, to plant potatoes and donate the organic harvest to the soup kitchen where once she volunteered. Where former coworkers can nod heads in mute respect and the homeless can yet again benefit from the unstinting gift of her person – her physical matter reconstituted – even as the other self – the soul – has slipped in Byron's words into "that dreamless sleep." How fitting. How exquisite, really, to be rendered into complex carbohydrates to nourish the weary and dispossessed on this earth, even after death, even as she had done in life, so that some residual aspect of her goodness might be resurrected from the eternal decease that passeth understanding and slapped onto plastic trays as dollops of mashed potatoes for the poor.

Plunk! Partake all ye gathered 'round of her goodness. Plop. So benevolent! Splat. A saint! But of a dear departed's saintliness, what more is there to say?

This: I don't *love* you. The third beat. Not love. Hinting that she harbors a sentiment unnamed, but the feeling is other than love. Hardly a surprise if that is her intended meaning, but what might the sentiment be if not love? Need? Yes, need.

She needs him for financial security and a purse stuffed with credit cards for reconnaissance at Nordstrom to finger apparel and splurge on the latest designs (never mind her money from Daddy invested for the grandkids in small- and mid-cap mutual funds). Or to buy a new wardrobe for her hubby as was required after the bonfire in the backyard and her glowering over the red-hot barrel with poker in hand while every stitch of fabric he ever owned – going back to college, to the military – went up in flames. Including his socks. "I'm sick to death of seeing these things of yours." Including socks. Her excuse, doubtless suggesting she is weary of him as well. Not love then, but need. Needing him. As she did in sixth grade while shooting poisonous remarks his way in lunch line or smacking him with a book after class when minding his own business. Putting a tack in his shoe once during gym. Until a boy asks his mother why would a girl behave so, and a mother laughs at her sixth-grade son. Deserve? No. Something different, she replies. The way it is with sixth-grade girls, she explains, though he never believes it. "Because she likes you." Likes him? Likes to slap or punch his side or shove him from behind as if every part of this body were contemptuous when he wants only to be left alone.

I don't love *you*. The fourth possibility. Not you. Meaning that she does indeed love, but someone else. Or something else. Yes, it is something else she loves. *Haute couture* and imported marble surfaces of the highest quality. Spices to corrode his soft tissue. Oregano to dissolve the organs. Heaps of oregano dumped onto breakfast potatoes when she knows he cannot tolerate seasoning of any sort because it triggers bouts of indigestion. Spiced to death out of spite, or is it wheat germ she has sprinkled on the fried potatoes this morning to address the "motility problem" about which she frets? What exactly is the flavor on his tongue and down his throat? Blood? Gunmetal. The slow burn. Never mind. Instead, he responds by throwing a knife more forcefully than is typical on a Sunday morning.

"Well I don't love you *either*."

Up, down, up.

Thump a-thump thump.

Back and forth until he hits the bullseye.

Her lips curl at the corners in a grin, or is it a sneer?

After 45 years, he still cannot be certain. Or is it 55?

"Did you even hear me?" This she asks because she knows – they both know – he is hearing impaired from afternoons of classical music, Mahler, with the volume cranked to turbojet amplitude, and more recently the genre called electronica.

He does not answer, so she says it a second time, referring to California poppies in the spring breeze like gold flakes suspended inches above the backyard slope. "I said 'I love our view'."

She circles the chair to place palms on his shoulders while gazing outside. Gives him a pat as he samples a savory potato, then another. "And don't be silly, because you know you do."

"Do what?"

"You love me." Her mouth is inches from his ear.

Very well, he admits to himself, feeling the comfort of her hands on his shoulders, sensing the desolation of life without her. I do love you. And no matter where the beat is placed this time, the old saw is all the more exasperating because it is true. The potatoes aren't bad either.

7. TED

Standing at reception, he slides the insurance card and thirty-dollar copayment across the counter before whispering an answer. How to circumvent self-diagnosis yet not sound the lunatic? Very well, Ms. What-Brings-You-In-Today. Pain, pluripotent pain. Is that the right modifier for migratory misery blossoming like adversarial stem cells on the ascent from nether regions?

Metastasis? Surgery? Who knew?

Thinking how it would have been decades past or might be in the future, so different from the present he once imagined. Knowing now. How things stand in the unimagined now, the unmanageable now with its stalls caused by a biological transmission burning from shifting gears. First gear, a subliminal malaise akin to predictive sensing of unconscious forces up to no good. Second gear, sputters protesting the grade. Third gear demons devouring the spirit of the digestive machine. Fourth gear efflorescence, a flowering of dragons attacking from the rear to frustrate further motion and disrupt... well... pretty much everything in his life. Problem was, he could offer none of it as evidence without mortification or mixing metaphors, without implying the difficulty simmers within his skull.

A ringing phone. Waiting for the gatekeeper to pick up and respond. Retrograde nudge of the insurance card. Not so much as a blink from Ms. I've-Heard-It-All-Before to acknowledge a life form undone.

Seeing two chairs unoccupied, but nothing on an end or in a quiet corner, Ted takes a center seat in the waiting area. The disagreeable design sprouts mono-arms with shared bends of metal forcing antisocial elbows tight against the torso.

He sheds an overcoat and shuffles over to a rack stuffed with pamphlets on the common cold versus influenza (compare and contrast, if you please), breast cancer and diabetes. Shingles. Quaint name, shingles, for a vile visitation. He selects a less-chafing *Family Circle* magazine and navigates back toward his seat while trying to filter out glances so difficult to ignore. Grandparents managing saplings, mothers with twenty-somethings too old but not too stupid to be living at home and carted to appointments. Seniors with leopard prints staining tissue-paper skin.

His legs stall at a photo screwed to the wall of a Dalmatian wearing a fire hat, the frame centered above an aquarium – an alignment suggesting water quenching flames? – just as a child behind his back coughs. Another kid to his left sneezes. Social facilitation? He holds his breath while following the sinusoidal undulations of a blue-and-red neon tetra in the fish tank. Tranquility expressed in motion. A domain exempt from fire, unless –

do fish catch colds as people do? He exhales. Is there escape from hydrodynamically driven contagion in a bowl? Impossible. Within and without the bowl, he envisions boundaries of water and air reshaping currents at greater and lesser scale, transferring pestilence, building a case for fractal epidemiology. People contracting colds or worse in a communal waiting room just like this one. Within the room, tropical fish in an aquarium catching colds in their collective soup; within the iridescent fish, microbes spreading colds through shared currents of interstitial fluid; inside the microbes...

He sits again as a door to the inner offices opens, and a foreign name is apparently mispronounced by the woman holding the door ajar. Apology offered and a second name called. A gang of three tropical fish cruises their artificial aqua-turf as he squirms for a comfortable position on the hard seat. Thumbing though the *Family Circle* magazine with a feature article on sugar skin peels increases his unease as each summoned patient prompts another bout of fidgets among the neglected. More throat clearing, hacking. A kid digs his nose and licks pickings from a finger. An urge suppressed to swat the brat. Get a grip, he tells himself. The thought *Our sins can make us stronger* roams the parietal lobe. Who said that? Knowing something to be wrong but wanting it anyway? Shameful. Fifteen minutes shot to hell.

Out of the corner of his eye, a toddler brachiates before testing the dynamics of upright locomotion. Holding the magazine higher to eliminate the distraction might... then again, no... within Ted's unwelcome field of peripheral vision the wobbler approaches ground zero. Some would think the effort adorable. Perhaps it is. He pictures a train wreck – one adult foot stationary across the toddler tracks, scalar intersecting vector – but whose problem was it, really? The option of simply taking no action, of doing nothing. Yes. That. The mental stall translates to the physical. The child clips his shoe and sprawls flat-faced on the tile. Wet wailing. A scowl from mother. Shameful. Delicious. The dirty look invites rebuttal, but to what purpose the well-aimed barb? Woman: mind thy charge and blamest not the stranger's footwear. Absurd to sputter so. A cell phone pulled from a pocket could defuse the situation, but no. Forbidden. A posted sign bars its use. *Strictly* forbidden, no less. Why the semantic pleonasm? Half an hour wasted. Forty...

"Mr. Timmult."

His name, more or less, is mispronounced not by the gatekeeper but by Madam Paperwork shuffling at reception. Furrow dead center between her eyebrows. A warning, this. Approach with caution.

He stands and aims for the demon eyebrows.

"We don't have up-to-date financial responsibility information. Please fill these out."

He glances at the paperwork rotated his way. "You've got my name spelled incorrectly."

Comment ignored. Try again. "My coverage has not

changed since last time."

Deaf ears. Pages secured to a clipboard along with chained pen, ensemble nudged another inch across the counter by a no-nonsense finger tap-tap-tapping in apparent irritation. Triplet taps repeated three times. Speak and be sent to the back of the bus. Refuse and risk being banished to the parking lot.

On the chair again with forms, wallet, and insurance card in hand to survey a landscape of blank lines. Something called "Plan Type." Insurance I.D. number, group number, individual number, HMO or PPO. He does what can be done and returns to the counter.

Madam Paperwork's index finger is held in the air and points at the ceiling for no apparent reason, nails painted lavender, he notices. Entries scrutinized line by line. Obvious dissatisfaction. "HMO, PPO, or EPO?"

"I don't understand the distinction."

"Well, we need to know."

Holding it. Holding it in. Not making a peep. (Again the stall: source or symptom of the problem?)

"Your insurance cards, please." Phony courtesy. Wiggling fingers as if he were five years old.

Mind swimming with rejoinders unspoken. You may have my firstborn if it pleases, madam. You may have all things above and beneath, but might not you have examined the insurance card you now require when it was offered initially? More useless mental sputters.

Heels clicking on floor tiles. Whirring of a copy machine. The card is returned wordlessly.

He must risk it. "Will this delay my being seen?"

"You will be called."

Ms. Personality.

Back to a seat in limbo-land. Watching plaster on the wall for fifty-five minutes. Forty-five years of...

"Mr. Timmult."

He rises, wincing, follows through the open door a fast-stepping girl in a skirt and white smock – short smock and super-short skirt – far too bare and young for a nurse's aide, if that is her title. Politically incorrect of course to think "girl," but what else suits so perfectly? Down a hall pronto to room 7.

He hangs his coat on a peg as she slaps the examination table with a palm. *Down boy*. Paper crinkling under the pressure of settling thighs while his mouth gapes to accept as a baby robin the disposable thermometer.

"Blood pressure."

Thoughts of unfeathered hatchlings expectant in a nest. Vulnerable lives. On the brink.

A jerk of her head. "Sweater please."

"Oh, sorry." He removes the sweater and feels the pressure cuff around his biceps as unanticipated proximity – his bare arm, her lips, that cleavage – wrecks any effort to prevent a regular respiratory rhythm from cascading into self-conscious gasps. She gives him a curious look while removing the cuff and thermometer. Notes scribbled. A sexual harassment suit in the making? Tears.

He panted at me Your Honor. Six months, with no parole.

"Remove your trousers."

Looking up at her. Startled. "What?"

"Remove your pants. Doctor'll be in shortly."

The doctor isn't. Chart on the wall of twenty do's and don'ts unless heart disease at an early age is your cup of tea, you fool. Stainless-steel kidney tray, forceps (for what purpose?), three boxes of latex gloves. Glass canister with cotton, another canister three-quarters full of sterile blue solution. Cooties prohibited here. Strictly, one hopes, yet there are scratching noises somewhere within the walls. Street mice pilfering narcotics? No reading material in sight. Time passing, passing, until rodent-like scraping the other side of the door too high above the floor for a mouse. Ah, yes, at last. A folder is removed, papers are flipped, the door swings wide. Whoosh of a white lab coat. Seat taken on the swivel stool. Laptop placed on counter and top flipped open with seamless and highly practiced maneuvers, oddly comforting.

"Theodore."

"Ted," Ted corrects as the physician fixes focus on the computer monitor.

"Mmm. So what brings you in today, Theodore?"

So much for doctor-patient rapport. Uncertainty revived as to what might be medically relevant (yet not sound the demented hypochondriac: Devils down below, Doc, blasting caps in my belfry, so give it to me straight. *Stage four, you say? Only a week to live?*) Cancel that. The less theatrical, the better. Pain. Disruption. Getting worse. No relief.

"Mmm." Scrolling computer files flickering illumination from the doctor's reflective lenses. "You were in just about this time last year."

"Is that right?"

"Yes. The year before as well. Same time of year."

"Oh yes? Well I..."

I, what? And so what of past visits?

"How long did you say you've had the pain?"

He dials back. A week or two, not three. He puts it out there for the expert.

Text is typed into a medical database automatically updating master files in the cloud. "Two weeks then?"

"Sounds right."

"External or internal?"

"Ah, internal." Is that right? "And external." Where was the dividing line?

Fingernails clicking on the keyboard. Manicured. "Let's take a look." Gloves snapped on.

Sweat. Dry sanitary paper sticking to palms and face and genitals. Probing. A Question.

"Diet?"

"Meat. Mostly."

"Mmm. Sit up please. Lettuce? Broccoli?"

"Don't much care for that. Meat though."

"How about vegetables?"

He ponders. Potatoes are a vegetable, no? "I like

French fries."

"Anything you've been doing differently? Stress. Change of diet?"

He thinks about his wife, Lavinia. Her good old Ted, the Swiss-watch reliable hubby. His life. Hadn't joined a gym yet, though he still carries in the wallet a coupon for a club not more than a mile's drive that advertises chrome-plated equipment with flat-screen displays. Birthday gift certificate from somebody who cares more than they should. Hasn't the time and probably too late now anyway. Quit smoking, sort of. Longer work hours. Bed after the late-evening news then back to the office to sit in a chair all day. Little exercise. Well, none, really. Apprehension. Thoughts of mortality.

"Nothing I can think of."

The doctor closes the laptop and swivels to face his patient. "Regular?"

"Not so much." An insipid expression he's heard too often from his almost-teenage boys. Why use it? Think, then talk. Or don't talk.

"Thanksgiving."

Neither a question nor a diagnosis. What to say?

Prompt repeated in imperative mode (or is it mood?) by the man with the degrees on the wall. "Tell me about your Thanksgiving."

Small talk? OK. He describes the long weekend. Relatives flying down on Wednesday and hanging around for cheap flights back home after the Sunday rush. Brother Gene and the screaming kids plus the scary oldest boy. Well, man now. Sister-in-law no help with anything. Spoiled bunch. Mom and Pop up from Florida to see the grandkids, both tolerable until their third highball. First signs of dementia in Mom; second or third in Pop. Worries about things to come in that department plus past-due college tuition bills rolling in with two more kids to follow if they didn't start shooting heroin first. New job to pay for everything, and maybe that was part of it too. Disappearing into work, sinking deeper into the pit of assurance that any meaning in work or play has only to do with others. Their needs and wants. Family first and all that.

"Demons," the doctor says.

"Beg pardon?"

"You're talking about your demons."

"Did I say that?"

"Not surprising you have headaches and the rest. How do you cope?"

Cope? He doesn't cope; he avoids. Goes down to the basement to tinker on the workbench if people don't come tagging along after him, which they inevitably do, then sneaks out to the garage until someone barges in to kick up dust and mess with something and break it. Heated discussions in the kitchen about cable TV or dumb politicians or recycling or something. Escapes behind a locked door in the upstairs bathroom to read on the can for a delicious hour. Wife's idea of an en suite haven. Big remodel costing thousands and still paying for it. Longer work hours. What the heck.

"Stay off it." The physician's lower lip droops disapproval. Or droops something.

"Off what?"

"Don't spend time sitting in there. A few minutes maximum."

"I read Huck Finn."

"What do you mean?"

"I reread *Huckleberry Finn* in there. In the bathroom, I mean, over Thanksgiving weekend."

"The entire book? Great Scott!"

He chuckles. "Great Twain."

"Well don't do that." No amusement in the professional voice. "Manage your stress some other way. I can give you a prescription for anxiety or an anti-inflammatory, but – "

"Yes?"

"Relax but don't dilly-dally in the bathroom. No straining. No reading. Havoc if you do, the very devil. Use the cortisone sparingly." Scribbled Rx handed over.

"Would surgery be – ?"

"Used to do that on occasion, the old timers anyway. Don't any more except for extreme cases. Inflammation comes back unless you change your habits."

"Aha." Inflammation. Pathology. The dragons.

"Good to take psyllium every day. Over the counter. Soft pads with witch hazel."

Prescription folded in half. "OK. Anything else?

The physician is halfway out the door. "Potato isn't a vegetable."

"It isn't?"

"No. Tuber. Eat more lettuce."

Hour-and-twenty-minute wait for a five-minute consultation with a two-hundred-dollar tab. Lots of lettuce and more life to live. Modern medicine.

8. LAVINIA

Family. A daughter's relationship on the brink. A husband obsessed with a dead cousin decades after an apparent wrong is perpetrated when the two boys were kids. A gun-loving nephew with a maniacal streak. An uncle locked away in some security ward for one – possibly two – deaths. In-laws coping with the onset of Alzheimer's.

A box of cotton swabs, the larger count of 500 she prefers, lay open on the tile counter with a half dozen spilled out next to a small, rectangular mirror of the sort women carry in handbags. Adjacent to the mirror, a credit card aligns perfectly with a tile's white grout. From the oven, a hint of cinnamon and apple perfumes the air. Bent over at the waist in the adjacent family room, she grabs another cushion and then wiggles into a slow waltz with the fabric, stroking each of the six cushion surfaces, coaxing microfiber into neat rows of nap as the rotary motor emits a comforting suction sound to which Lavinia has become accustomed. A happy sound, she decides. The look is ephemeral but pleasing to her eyes as she reaches for the last cushion and hums a tune. Even the noise of the high-tech vacuum is to her liking except for the problem of ringing phones and doorbells going unanswered. Lavinia smiles, high on the brilliance of morning light and fragrance of cinnamon and comfort of freshly scrubbed surfaces, until she stops. A hesitation is apparent in her manner, head up and on the lookout.

The doorbell? She flips the rocket-vacuum motor off and makes her way to the living room with its sectional sofa, where a chaise end has been dragged back a few feet in preparation for vacuuming underneath. Something is amiss, but what? She drags the furniture another foot and stops a second time. Yes. The doorbell.

Lois sweeps into the room in Betty Davis fashion and dumps a shopping bag onto the nearest chair. "My lord, girl, you're moving furniture to clean?"

Lavinia smiles. "Tidying up, yes."

"Only you, sweetness. You're the only person in this entire town who would lug furniture around to get at crumbs where there are no crumbs." But the visitor is already on her way into the kitchen, opening the refrigerator as if it were her own. Her back is momentarily turned as Lavinia pulls a cabinet drawer open and sweeps the mirror and credit card into it with a single motion of the wrist.

"And what is that heavenly aroma?"

"Apple turnovers for the boy's lunches tomorrow."

"Of course. The only two boys in school who bring gourmet lunches from mom to the cafeteria. It's so — Stepford!"

A furrow dents Lavinia's forehead midway between her eyes.

"But don't mind me, sweetness. It's just the envy talking. Got any coffee?"

"I'll make fresh."

They chat as the coffee drips.

An hour after setting two cups on the sideboard to drain, Lavinia steers her SUV along suburban streets before reaching the commercial section of town where warehouses outnumber other buildings. She drives across railroad tracks, turns into a dead-end alley where an abandoned building grins at her passing, darkened from a momentary overcast, the harbinger of autumn. Lavinia parks the car, rings the bell adjacent to a metal security gate, and glances up at the three-story tenement midway down the alley.

He offers a line for a boob touch. She shakes her head at the suggestion but smiles and allows his hand to travel down a bit further, and stops it as it slips just south of navel territory. It is seductive to be here, she knows, dangerous. Sick, really. What she is doing is stupid and against the law. It is more fun than anything else she has ever done before. It must stop. Tomorrow.

At home that evening during the dinner party, Lavinia darts into the guest bathroom after excusing herself to "powder her nose." When she returns to the table, Ted catches her eye and touches his upper lip. She responds by brushing away a trace of white residue.

★

A suggestion of something amiss brought Sarah short after she lit the lamp and dumped kindling into the wood box. Trailing down from the double-hung, as if someone had nudged open the upper pane during the night, several feet of blue cotton fabric had been wedged from inside and the window pushed closed again. Sarah knew at once the apron string belonged to her sister, the only female in the family who could complete such precision stitchwork by hand, finishing hems so perfectly that anyone would be inclined to think the sewing had been done by an expert on a machine.

Sarah stoked the fire and filled two pots of water for boiling before setting table for breakfast. Hearing footfalls on the stairs, she glanced from the stove only long enough to whisper, "Good morning," as her mother entered the kitchen. She would not mention the apron string, nor would her mother say a word that morning because they knew. They both understood. Her three brothers and father who stomped in from the barn, one after the other, squinted in the direction of the window to make apparent the fact that each had encoded the strap, nothing more. Only after the men drained the last from their cups and cleared the room did Sarah catch the expression on her mother's face, one she had observed over the years when difficulties, or "signs" of potential trouble, as elders put it, presented themselves. The familiar set to the jaw and... what might a person call it? Resignation. No one mentioned her older sister that morning, or more to the point, her sister's absence from the meal. No one would speak her name during the coming week. Or month.

The kitchen window, three times taller than wide, allowed occupants of the house visual access to the awakening countryside each winter sunrise during breakfast, but this morning something about the view unsettled both women as they tidied up. Suggestions of an escape route and desperation. The house had been built between English neighbors on either side and between the town of Charm, dozens of miles to the southeast, and West Salem in the opposite direction, but it was situated much closer geographically and in other ways to West Salem. If one were to consign local scenery around Charm to canvas, the image would do justice to a country calendar – in the style of Grandma Moses or Currier and Ives – with draft horses hauling hay wagons, buggies riding high on wooden wheels, hills dotted with white barns stacked almost one atop another, orderly fields, orderly folks, lawns with flowerbeds in summer and snowmen in winter. Horses pulled buggies around West Salem as well, but the terrain here settled flatter and muddier, giving in to an exhaustion that nudged buildings slightly askew on weary ground. Sarah's house, orderly outside and within, felt anything but firm this winter morning, as if the foundation were slipping.

★

Straight from vending machines at the bus depot, the snacks on Lavinia's lap had been purchased on impulse after she'd passed up a rubbery-looking breakfast available at the airport, prompting her to settle for bottled water and something resembling a sticky bun plus a packet of cheese and crackers. The items were wrapped in high-tech cellophane that resisted fingers and teeth. One bite of the bun after settling down in the bus seat dampened her appetite enough that she swept the purchases, wrappers and all, into a plastic bag and vanquished the bag into the big compartment of her purse.

Lavinia had known better than to request a ride from the airport – hadn't asked for the favor because of her brother in law, Marshall – but simply gave her sister the estimated hour of arrival according to the timetable. With a half hour to go before her appearance in West Salem, Lavinia dug in a coat pocket for the iPhone, surmising in advance the device would fail to provide service for text messages out here in the boonies. With suspicions confirmed, she popped a bud into each ear and pulled up the TED Talk that had piqued her interest the previous weekend. The video was not one she would have downloaded without urging from a friend: something to do with the moral roots of political views and far too esoteric for her temperament, Lavinia reminded herself. Still, after a first viewing, some phrases kept percolating in her head, and who would have thought? Now she wanted to check the assertion about conservatives having five-channel morality and liberals having two channels. Did it matter? For the big picture, possibly; in personal terms, hardly.

As far as politics were concerned, Lavinia's interests extended just far enough to carry her to the polls once a year. Voting was a civic duty, and that had always felt like enough. She was a moderate, or rather more on the modern or liberal cusp, she supposed, if anyone cared, but no one would even raise a topic like that in her progressive community back home. Recyclers, social justice enthusiasts, and, yes, tree huggers all: pretty much everyone in her sphere fit the picture.

But here? More troubling prior to departure were emotional prospects associated with this leg of the trip. Of immediate concern was how the terrain outside the bus window might trigger uneasy memories after decades lived in exile halfway across the country. Lavinia pressed back against the headrest to focus her thoughts. She decided to replay the start of the TED lecture. Yes, she had remembered accurately at least one thing about the talk: the claim that both liberals and conservatives shared a pair of moral concerns. Number one: minimizing harm to others, akin to the physician's credo. Number two: promoting fairness. She closed her eyes, thinking these two dispositions – optimistic propositions about politics – had much in common; merge the two ideals and you had something reminiscent of the Golden Rule. Perhaps that was the way to remember this part of the lecture since nearly everyone on earth believed in "Do unto others." In theory if not practice.

The road wound along a river for miles then ascended forested banks that gave way to farmland, gray-brown this time of year except for snow-bank signatures in shady spots. After a jolt by the driver who took a curve too fast and swerved to avoid hitting something on the road, Lavinia glanced out the window. The bus settled again. Familiar landmarks now started to mix it up with unexpected scenes as the bus zipped down the old highway, carrying her to a reunion that had been delayed for nearly a decade owing to children and family. Such was life at mid-life. At least that was the excuse she allowed herself. She pressed the pause button on her phone as familiar property lines whizzed by. Rows of oak and maples created access lanes to otherwise inaccessible fields, just as she remembered, something like the hedgerows in Normandy. Some of the rows consisted of pine trees that had been handed out by the thousands as seedlings during those decades when soil conservation was a flourishing enterprise. She remembered very well, in fact had planted her share. Now a rusting refrigerator lay next to the mailbox of a once-thriving Western Reserve estate, its orchard a tangle of dead limbs. Massive barns that had dominated for a century every other feature of the landscape continued to do so, but today some of the buildings lay splintered on the ground. Exceptions were those maintained by the community of friends, structures Lavinia recalled from back in the days when she would ride the school bus down side roads to a then newly consolidated high school built in the middle of a cornfield. Strange to think of that building – so contemporary looking at first and out of place in its rural setting – as being some thirty years old now. The look, feel, way sunlight struck the landscape, all were just as she remembered yet somehow drearier this morning, or was it she who had grown jaded?

Here and there, bulldozers had scraped the ground to catch runoff from fields in ponds more numerous than she remembered. Midwestern folks liked their swimming holes for a summer dip, or a turn at fishing. Well, some did. Then came the scattered homesteads belonging to the community of friends, each place distinctive for a lack of distinction emblematic of a people notorious for their aversion to distinction. Unadorned buildings, single-panel curtains hung straight down from one side of tall windows and – the giveaway to anyone familiar with the territory – the absence of power lines from road to buildings. Plain as the nose on your face who lived in those places.

*

After dinner, Lavinia prepared coffee as her sister set two glasses on the table next to a bottle of cognac. Millie had added a few inches to her waistline after the third child but otherwise appeared to have maintained health and humor. The same could not be said of Millie's husband

who wilted into recumbency each evening while down-
ing a six pack and staring at a television invariably tuned
to a local station featuring nonstop "breaking news."
Not a bad fellow, considering. "I like that station because
it's unbiased," he'd remarked. Not a bad fellow though,
Marshall, Lavinia reminded herself, even if his idea of
news took the form of one hyped-up moral crisis after
another. Just now the TV anchorman pitched a plea to
the "infected" youth of America, warning his audience
how tattoos violated the sanctity of the human body.
The anchor introduced a pair of Christian rockers who
had opted to undergo painful laser removal after botched
ink jobs, tears moistening flushed, young cheeks aquiver
at the retelling.

When they'd embraced, the sisters had agreed to a
pact. No blame games this time. No touchy subjects this
first evening and, above all, nothing to do with husbands
or the minefield of parents. On this initial evening together, they would share cognac and celebrate old times,
gossip about former schoolmates and crushes, smile over
who had ended up marrying whom, who had prospered
or failed. Better to giggle than whimper, they agreed. In
negotiating this reunion, Lavinia felt immune to criticism
anyway after twenty plus years of marriage to her high
school sweetheart and a couple of decades spent pursuing
the antithesis of a career-centered path, exactly as she'd
anticipated.

They reminded one another of cousins and former teachers, chatted about shady merchants and pious preachers. Then in passing, Lavinia brought up the neighbor who had worked as handyman for the sisters' family when a broken something-or-other needed attention, and their father had neither time nor inclination to do the job himself. White-whiskered Dan, patriarch of the clan next door and jack-of-all-trades, had died years before, according to Millie, leaving the buildings and acreage to his oldest son who now had two daughters and three boys of his own, each of marrying age. Indeed, the oldest daughter was somewhat past that age. Millie hesitated in mid-sentence. One might use the horrid expression, "old maid," she added, but something to do with the matter clearly upset Millie who went silent until Lavinia pressed for details.

It was such a shame about the oldest daughter next door. Millie explained how the girl had fallen for a boy from the more progressive community of Charm, a lad of the same faith as the girl's family, but with parents so much more prosperous and educated than hers that he might have come from Mars. The boy had graduated high school, made himself computer literate, and taken a job as a computer designer in a cabinet-making shop. And while each of those qualities might have been viewed by most parents as desirable, they were abhorrent to the father next door whose religious convictions remained doggedly fixed. The daughter had been forced to quit school in sixth grade, was never allowed a say when it came to choosing friends, and had been passed over by every boy her father deemed suitable from within the straight-laced and sparsely populated West Salem community. In the end, the father would never approve his daughter's choice of an outsider, and she would lose her family if she insisted on following her heart. In her parent's mind, the girl might have been "taken" by any man as long as the suitor came from the family's own sect (their own "people") and did the initiating. In the daughter's mind, her lot was the curse of the unchosen, deprived of voice and choice. All the young woman's days had been spent in isolation until love arrived. Indeed, mutual love, but to secure that love she must lose her family.

Lavinia tipped the bottle of cognac to top off both glasses. "What do you mean by 'lose'?"

"Well you just *know* the family would have to disown her. Remember what those folks practice? Shunning. Nothing's changed around here since back when we were kids."

Lavinia remembered. Any member of the faith who willfully violated one of the cardinal rules of the church or countered family authority ran the risk of being rendered dead to the community for all intents and purposes.

"Can you imagine?" Millie mused.

"No – what?"

"I mean a daughter treating her parents that way after all they'd done for her. That poor mother."

Mother? The mother? Lavinia felt her face go warm but sipped cognac and kept opinions to herself.

★

Sometime before sunrise she awakened with a start. Lavinia stared into the darkness, listened, then rose. She slipped from the guest room into the hall to investigate what might have disturbed her slumber and discovered the source at once. People down the hall were talking, but she recognized none of the voices. She could see the door of her sister's bedroom standing ajar and tip-toed closer to see that a bedside television had been left on. Millie lay on her side facing the wall opposite a snoring husband, blue-white light flickering on both bodies, still as corpses. Lavinia waited for movement but could detect neither the rise nor fall of breathing. They might have been drugged, freeze-dried, turned to stone next to a TV tuned to the station that had been on the evening before and continued to squawk in the small hours. She imagined sound waves bouncing off bedroom walls, penetrating curtains and seeping into rugs, into brains, "balanced" human interest stories about rediscovered faith, socialism undermining decisions in the nation's capital, the hoax of climate change, evils of abortion and same-sex liaisons and immigration, and the lie of evolutionary theory.

★

The first time it happened, she tried to think how long it must have been: ten years at least, maybe twenty. She traced images backwards through time, measured in decades, of municipal buses and dime store lunch counters, of policemen with attack dogs barring entry to schools. Perhaps it was the lull of the late-afternoon hour that prompted her to reconsider while menfolk in the living room hooted at a Sunday football game. It came so unexpectedly that Lavinia had misgivings about whether she'd even heard the term spoken aloud. Besides, no one else in her sister's house seemed to have noticed anything. What could she do about it anyway, this monochromatic language? Raise a stink? When it happened a second time, the word followed guttural modifiers.

"Godammed stupid ni***r!"

Not the phrase itself but the echo of the word carried Lavinia back to an era of bullets and little girls lying dead in church. But here? Now, in whitewashed middle America? In her own family? She eavesdropped on banter from the living room. Her in-laws were decent enough people – everyone agreed – with the man of the house something of a local celebrity for being the most vocal fan at sporting events, the most supportive and generous with time and money, especially at local high school basketball and football games despite his youngest boy graduating years before. Vocal as well during NFL telecasts, screaming or moaning, depending on the score. Now, apparently displeased with a failed third-down play together with the traitorous behavior of one of the home-team linebackers in real life, it was more than Marshall could bear. Why didn't the guy go back where he came from?

That guy. *That ni★★★r.*

It wasn't language so much as the anger that caused Lavinia to wonder from where it came, this rage at certain athletes and single moms. Outrage at college "imbeciles." Stupid gorillas on the make and take. At everyone "not us." Why the wrath when Marshall had been handed essentially everything a person could want in life? Good parents and a stable home when growing up. Physical strength and health, making him a big frog in a little puddle. Steady employment, the love of a reliable woman, and great kids. Why the resentment?

From the kitchen, Lavinia might have peered into the living room by leaning forward an inch or two but opted instead to shift her gaze out the window that framed neighboring farm buildings while her mind raced back in time. Virtually every statement from Marshall since she'd walked in the door carried negative overtones, mirroring ideas on the television station about "kids" these days. No respect, any of them. College jackasses smoking dope all day, every day. People in welfare lines sucking the nation's economy dry. Education a joke for fools wasting their time on stupid crap instead of working for a living and doing something productive. Life lived bulls-eye center amidst the ruins. Obscene propane and fuel prices for working people, do-nothing foreigners out there swamping emergency rooms, illegals breeding like bunnies. Failed public schools, urban gangs, abortion mills, and the liberal media and courts ruining the country. Football players abandoning home teams for the almighty dollar. No loyalty anywhere these days, no values.

GD Stupid Ni***rs! Whatever happened to family? To faith? To decency?

Sitting on a kitchen chair that faced the window, Lavinia's mind revisited the Internet talk on her iPhone, the idea that people differed in their openness to experiences according to the lecturer – according to this Jonathan Haidt fellow, whoever he was. A liberal-minded person could be characterized as more open, he maintained, the conservative type more closed to new experiences. But the far more unexpected proposal was that conservatives nurtured three additional roots of morality compared to liberals, the extras centered on the perceived importance of loyalty, authority, and purity in their lives. Three concepts that liberals cared little about, or perhaps just a little less.

Was it true that people could be categorized this way, or was the idea another generalization? Didn't this kind of thinking smack of type theory? Back in college, Lavinia recalled being warned about such theories, notorious for failing to do what they claimed.

And what did it signify anyway: to hear that vulgar expression used again in the context of disloyalty? Loyalty had a familiar ring in this household, applied with a sort of panicked urgency. Loyalty to one's own. To one's family, one's community, one's team. Her own sister's endorsement of the neighboring parents' expectations, a mother's right to loyalty trumping a daughter's feelings, no matter how heartfelt. A husband's allegiance to his kids' high school teams and tirades against *those fuckers* who quit home teams to make millions by switching affiliation.

Authority and respect for "our own kind" were equally important around these parts. Lavinia pictured household TV sets tuned to a single station harping on narrow themes and variations. Outrage over food stamps rather than corporate fraud despite costs associated with one overshadowing the other by powers of ten. Or a hundred. Laws of the land purportedly on the brink of collapse. People confronting the police. Protests. Kneeling. The Good Book ignored.

Another regional mantra: purity, in the sense of deference to the blessing of our bodies that must never be violated. Sacred bodies demeaned by tattoos, abortion, pot smoking: each one a sickness of the soul.

On a typical day during her ordinary life back home with Ted, matters of this sort would have had little potency for Lavinia. Indeed, for as long as she could remember, she had laughed at the idea of authority, had switched allegiance to a political party more than once, had quit her sorority after two years, rebounded from an abortion with fleeting misgivings, smoked weed now and then along with use – or overuse if truth be told – of other recreational drugs, and paid for a petite heart to be inked on her backside to commemorate a sense of personal liberation, even if that freedom were more imagined than real. Certainly Lavinia's instincts took the form of two-channel morality rather than five, favoring the ideas of care for others and fairness, the Golden Rule shared by liberals and conservatives alike, or by any human of good conscience.

But honestly, who gave a hoot one way or the other, Lavinia asked herself this Sunday afternoon in the kitchen of her sister's overheated rural house. An in-law's gutter language was just so much verbal phlegm to be ignored, was it not? Two or five beliefs underlying one's political alignment, or a baker's dozen: what of it? Yet part of her did care, and she could not let the thought go. How could Millie tolerate such language in her house?

Millie laughed at the idea. Laughed in Lavinia's face while suggesting that "everybody lighten up." Nobody intended anything by those expressions, she maintained, and even if that were not the case, even if something mean were intended, no one was likely to change anyone's mind around here. "It's just words," Millie insisted, and one word was as good as another around here; didn't Lavinia remember that? The topic was too silly to talk about, but if Lavinia really needed to know, it wasn't colored people Marshall was referring to in that way anyway. He wasn't the least bit racist. Not at all. He was just referring to stupid people with that old expression. Really stupid people.

Lavinia swallowed hard. Was it possible to double down on bigotry so casually? She made a throat-clearing noise to mask emotion and dropped the subject while reminding herself that this branch of the family put as much stock in debate as in abstract art. What mattered to them was being down-to-earth, true and honest, unpretentious and never taken for a ride. Above all, what counted was a person's character: that was the real deal, when character meant fidelity to our kind of people in our kind of place because everything else everywhere else was likely to be phony or unworthy.

Only they would never admit to holding such opinions because they did not know they held them. Not consciously.

Lavinia grabbed her coat from the hall closet and stepped out the front door for a walk to clear her head. No matter, the biting cold, she said when her sister's eyebrows went north.

It was that hour around sunset on a clear winter evening when the sky fades from blue to steel gray, half-bright with unordinary light. She headed down the walkway toward the road, relieved to absent herself from people – her people, all people – if only for a few minutes, until she noticed someone else moving in the same direction, a face almost invisible inside a cape, a female stepping quickly toward the road.

Lavinia nodded as the stranger nodded back while glancing only for an instant into Lavinia's eyes as though it were improper to look too closely at another person, just as it was improper to peer too long into a mirror. Neither woman spoke, but there was something in the evening itself, in the silence and cold air, something about the young woman's expression, so plain and innocent and devoid of falsehood. To speak would have been an intrusion on the silver sliver of daylight remaining.

Lavinia felt her coat pocket and withdrew two pieces of hard candy, butterscotch. She reached out and offered one to the neighbor's youngest daughter in lieu of words, for that was who it must be, the daughter remaining at home. The girl shook her head while glancing at her own house as if someone might be watching, the movement surreptitious because she had already been reprimanded once this week for improperly fastening her bonnet, a violation judged as willful disregard of a conformity principle enforced by church deacons. So, too, the consumption of sweets. But Lavinia knew nothing of bonnets or deacons as the girl opened her mailbox and withdrew a thin letter, the first piece of mail that Sarah had received in her name in a year. Later in her bedroom under the light of a kerosene lamp, she would read the post office origin and a message from her older sister that would begin with a few reassuring lines necessitated after cutting apron strings.

Dear Sister Sarah, I fear you will be worried where I am now but know I am well. I know you are not allowed to write me, but remember that I will always love you and everyone in our family. Please tell each of them so...

But that came later. For now, Lavinia stands in the driveway of her sister's house and regards a young woman poised to walk away – neither individual is quite ready to go indoors – when it occurs to Lavinia that the plain people she grew up with as neighbors – those fully invested in the Amish philosophy, for there was no investment of the sort other than a complete one – embody precisely the three extra moral elements characterized in the TED lecture she has been replaying on the iPhone and in her mind for several days. Every aspect of their lives remained centered on *loyalty* to their own kind, respect for *authority*, and *purity* of mind and body. Still another descriptor came to mind. Conformity. Conform or be lost and shunned by the faithful, by family. Forever.

It also occurs to Lavinia as she and the neighbor girl turn to head toward their separate homes, that each residence in the vicinity represents a community of the like-minded, Lavinia's home no less than her sister's or the neighbor's, where one would see faces of only pale flesh tones, hear sounds with only reinforcing overtones, hold onto faith in propositions that stood on wobbly but unchallenged legs. That Marshall and her sister, along with other family members still living in the county in which they had been reared, within a cultural cocoon only a stone's throw from the houses in which they had been born, lived not just miles – light years, really – distant from her geographically and disconnected from Lavinia's way of thinking, but some were also halfway down the philosophical road to plain people, caught forever en route to a mailbox with the possibility of genuine news of a real and diverse world. Reaching out in various ways but never grasping much to do with that world. Tuned in always to a single channel and keeping a firm hold on beliefs and values, innocence and naivety, ignorance and purity. And if that were so, was it tragedy or cause for rejoicing?

9. LAVINIA

Lavinia's return trip through Cleveland includes a weekend visit with cousins who long ago opted to stick it out where ancestors from Eastern Europe found their first jobs in steel mills and a cigar factory. Although the Flats area tailgating the Cuyahoga River no longer belches soot, her second- and third-generation relatives have hunkered down to live their lives these days under mostly ashen skies even as Lavinia joined multitudes of her generation to escape the rust belt's overcast. The visit is pleasant if uneventful.

Lavinia has retained her figure and stands as tall as any female in a room. She scans the unoccupied waiting area in the airport terminal now and selects an end seat in a row of vinyl-clad chairs joined at the armrests. Absorbed in an Alice Munro story, she pays little mind when a man of indeterminate nationality takes the chair immediately on her left rather than any of a hundred unoccupied seats. He does not speak and seems hardly to breathe. Before she realizes what is happening, the man takes hold of her carry-on luggage and rotates the bag so that the zippered front faces his direction. Lavinia surmises that he has taken this action to allow himself more legroom.

In a single motion, he tilts her bag at a 45 and unzips the main compartment so that its front flap flops downward, exposing contents. She inhales a quiver when he extends a palm and slips it under the top blouse of her wardrobe – a shimmering silk affair worn once during her trip – until it is repositioned to exactly align atop her other clothes. He pats the front of the blouse so that it lays flat and unwrinkled, pats it as if it were an obedient puppy, but apparently notices one tip of the collar folded under, resembling a floppy ear. He straightens the collar point with thumb and fingertip and zips the bag closed. Her pulse is rapid when he rises from the chair. He walks away, total elapsed time half a minute.

Lavinia's half-empty flight back home is eventually announced over the public address system. Passengers roll bags toward the gate while checking that boarding passes are in hand. She has the luxury of an unoccupied seat next to hers on the relatively short flight back to her hometown where Ted will be waiting with the car.

Above the clouds, she thinks about the boy who spoke too quietly or flamboyantly in fourth grade and was trounced in the schoolyard during a recess one morning. She remembers a co-ed in the dorm three doors down from her room who had been hauled into some bushes on her way back one night from the library. She recalls the graceless facade of a local bank that gambles futures markets with the paltry savings of residents while refusing loans to local businesses and working families because interest rates on such investments are lower than other profit margins.

"They are the same," Lavinia says aloud to no one.

PART TWO

10. TED AND...

Mother and brother's bodies painted head-to-toe were left uncollected by the garbage truck on trash day. "You need to call the office, buddy." The driver hollered out the window at the man shivering curbside, breath from inside the vehicle escaping chapped lips in a fog of condensed condescension. "That there's a special pickup."

Neighbors wrapped in scarves had walked their dogs on the sidewalk in front of the property all morning and during much of the afternoon. Pets strained at leashes, but no one thought to look more closely. Residents on the block later claimed they assumed the objects left to rot at the edge of the street were mannequins or the like that had been collecting dust over the years. At least that was the rationalization offered for why they had failed to identify two community residents occupying the same house for more than four decades. It had been bitter cold that day. The bodies were not rotting but already partly frozen, and no one recognized the faces under what looked like whiteface and turned out to be spray-on latex paint (an off-white color charmingly labeled Swiss Coffee).

A steady progression of cars trolled the address that night after crime units arrived and departed and the corpses were "bagged and hauled away," as the local television station put it. On the evening news, Ted watched the alleged perpetrator, the oldest son, caught on camera in handcuffs, his head pushed down by an officer's palm while being shoved into the rear of a squad car. For the next week from suppertime to midnight, neighbors experienced frustration pulling out of driveways as a continuous stream of vehicles with rubbernecking occupants crept along what had been a peaceful street.

★

She tossed into conversations outdated concepts and commodities – duck butt, Wildroot Cream Oil – as if something about hair were relevant to the topic at hand and she'd been a flowerchild of the sixties. Silly expressions from as far back as the fifties peppered her dialogue, suggesting she'd seen too many Frankie Avalon flicks. That's a gas, Daddy-O. Crazy. She insisted that no one knew diddly about squat – squat in the present case referring to the heinous slaughter of a mother and brother – and from her first words in his presence, it seemed obvious he would not treasure her company over the long term.

Bottom line: he didn't believe a word she said. More precisely, he felt it generous to credit what she said with about 20% worth of belief against 80% disbelief. When they interacted – unavoidable given work assignments – it was as if opposing forces played tug-of-war with a riptide.

She fancied herself clever; his doubt surpassed cynicism. He believed he could detect a groping for ingenuity by the inadequate in the colleague.

Case in point. Once, with no context apparent, she claimed she didn't argue at night. During the daytime, yes, possibly, but not at night. Perhaps. Or did she?

"We don't argue until all hours of the night," were her exact words, but how should a person handle such a remark when "they" remained unspecified, and at least three interpretations were possible:

1. Emphasis on "until:" *they* only started arguing *late* at night.

2. Accent on "don't": *they* did *not* argue, period.

3. Taken as a whole: they argued some but *settled* things before the wee hours.

Ambiguous statements drove him crazy, and she was always saying such things. Writing copy like that as well. Correct interpretation? Who knew? Or cared for that matter.

"When did you stop shaving?" She pitched that remark at him after they met at a restaurant for a working lunch to discuss the double murder on Hanover Street, the most gruesome crime in the county in a decade. He had not stopped shaving of course, in fact had shaved every weekday morning since the age of about 14 promptly after waking up at 7 a.m. True, he'd inherited a genetic predisposition for dense facial hair and missed a morning now and then on a weekend or holiday, but she could not know that, and why would anyone bring up shaving over a business lunch in the first place? A working lunch to decide how to cover the trial, if an actual trial were held despite the likelihood that the perpetrator was deranged. Again, why her preoccupation with hair? And not just hair.

One morning she swiveled her desk chair and fluttered eyebrows in his direction, the seated equivalent of a twirl and curtsey. Then the punctuation mark. The dagger. "You look like a balloon in that outfit."

Taunt a fellow reporter who dressed superbly, who was praised as dapper by everyone else in the newsroom? To what end? Why would a person dream up personal insults when he was, and always had been, noted for a trim profile? The better course of course would have been silence, but he broke defensive wind. "I am... not... not..." Not what? His mind sputtered, voice faltered.

Back on the beat, he almost tripped over his shoes when she hollared at a man approaching from some distance down Hanover Street with a child in tow: "Your wife's son. Huh?" The implication seemed to be that the little boy was known to her. Or the father. Or both, and maybe that would have been amusing. Later, however, she admitted the two were strangers. For whose benefit, this performance then, when he'd been after an interview with a credible resident who might provide a soundbite for the next broadcast?

"We don't need to interview anybody around here," she asserted in the car. "There's no point. The guy's a paranoid schzophrenic, plain and simple." The "guy" being the son who had spray-painted his mom and older brother after slitting their throats in bed, then dragged the bodies out to the curb on trash-collection day. Apparently she fancied herself a psychiatrist as well as fashion critic. Her rueful smile suggested she had won again. High five to Ms. Insight. Groovy.

"It looks like you got your hair cut in an asylum." That was the wisecrack that sent things over the top as far as he was concerned. Along with her nonstop humming. True, he had decided to experiment with a new hairstyle. Yes, it might appear that someone had almost shaved his head below a bowl line on the sides, but the stylist did not use a bowl of any description, nor were the locks on top above the bowl line trimmed randomly. The spikiness was intentional, a contemporary look. Anything but cheap.

The flavor of bad karma, an odor of impertinence, weight of infuriating intrusion: these were the elements cluttering his mind each time he attempted in her presence to formulate a script for the next broadcast. The more he tried to ignore her, the more he couldn't get her scent and jabber and a sense of shifting gravity out of his head when she was around, so he decided it wasn't worth it. Time to punt. He put in a request to be reassigned, or to have her reassigned, and pressed the point for sanity's sake.

She cried. She wept in front of the suits. How could a person be so mean when all she ever wanted was a kind word from him? When they had been covering the big story together so well. Why would he make trouble for her like that? Why now, given a sensational double-murder story?

She proposed a meeting to "straighten things out." Just the two of them. He declined the invitation. She phoned during the evening, sent emails, posted a message on his Facebook page. When all else failed, she appeared on his doorstep, pounding the door with clenched fists late at night.

"Really?" He greeted her that way while standing at the foyer of his house with the front door and his mouth both wide open. "Really?"

"You leave me no choice." She looked a wreck. Her mouth and facial features conveyed the impression of a spooked pterodactyl. That was the image that popped into his mind as he took a step backward. Before he lost consciousness. Why a pterodactyl, he couldn't say exactly; maybe he had just run across an image of one online while surfing the Internet.

"May I come in?" This, the woman with a pistol pointed at his navel asked while standing on the doorstep.

The revolver, a small weapon of the sort some women

carry in a clutch handbag, caught a glint from the street-lamp. He noticed an index finger on the trigger as she waved the nose of the gun in a manner meant to herd him inside the entryway. Something she had seen in a B movie probably. Move it, Daddy-O. He took a step back while glancing up the street in hopes that a neighbor might be watching this absurd confrontation, might see enough to call the police, but the block appeared to be deserted, street-facing windows dark.

He had been reading an article that evening about happiness. The premise was that people can manufacture their own happiness by producing something called "synthetic happiness." Maybe that was why he found himself thinking about happiness now, or more to the point, contemplating too late the end of his life on Earth and any opportunity to grab hold of happiness, synthetic or otherwise.

The pterodactyl advanced. The last impressions to jangle 50-odd-billion occipital and temporal lobe neurons inside his skull that evening were a slight contraction of her trigger finger, the snap of a pistol's hammer striking a firing pin, and a world gone dark.

★

Their wedding coincided with the seventh game of the World Series, vows exchanged during the eighth inning, which accounted for a diversion of attention toward smart phones on the part of many males present. At the reception, a small gun – or what looked to be a gun and was in fact the very item she had brandished on his doorstep – replaced the more traditional replica of bride and groom atop a multilayered wedding cake. Many thought the joke in poor taste. Her intoxicated lesbian friend, an intimate since high school and thought by some to be "a little more than a friend," was asked to lower her voice and had to be escorted from the venue. Some family members speculated that the marriage would not last a season, but they were mistaken.

Ten years later, the son asked his mother about that initial marriage. It was not the first time his mom's relationship with his father came up along with queries as to what might have led to a divorce.

"Hard to say." The boy's mother frowned while retelling the tale of that night she had appeared at a fellow worker's house with a toy gun in hand. How everything changed after he recovered from the faint and found her dabbing his forehead with a damp washcloth. How they had looked into each other's eyes. Deeply. Him still breathing. Deeply. How she had predicted exactly what two court-appointed psychiatrists concluded, that the spray-paint murderer in the news back then was schizophrenic, paranoid schizophrenic. How he admitted that she had been right about so many things. And funny. And beautiful. With the voice of an angel.

"Those were his exact words, honey. 'The voice of an angel.'"

"Then why didn't you and Dad stay together?" the boy asked his mom.

"Why didn't the Donner party take the train?"

"Do you think you and Dad will ever patch things up?"

Her eyebrows went up. "I like to think only a closed mind is certain."

"Who said that?" the boy asked.

"A movie, honey. I heard it once in a movie."

11. TED'S DAUGHTER

In the hour before indigo dusk when the sun circumscribing a late winter afternoon declines at the double. Before a couple emotionally decouples. Upon exiting modern dance workshop and sprinting to catch a bus back to her flat and the master carpenter with stained glass eyes and a severed finger – hazard pay for one careless day, he jokingly dubs the disarticulated digit. Once the decision is made to challenge him. After the key to the apartment is turned and a greeting carries down the hall from her loveable lug, home from a job earlier than expected. Only when she joins him on the sofa and decides most bases are covered: should he resist, she will insist; start to veer and she'll re-steer; stall or balk and she'll make him talk all the more.

While endlight plays counterpoint for two, sitting close enough to press chiseled shoulder to meaty arm, devotees of truth or truths derived independently, she rises to admit slivered light through the blinds and retrieves the canvas. Hands it over and asks for honest thoughts about the most impassioned work she has done in a year. Prompts the man of sawdust and sweat for reactions though he distains questions that ride the coattails of implied questions.

He inclines across the painting to express interest or feigned interest then shifts to the customary angle of repose she knows well enough. Sighs a familiar sigh but does not resist. Does not veer. Does not stall. She watches as his arm is flexed to sweep the good hand just above surface oil, careful not to soil, and observes his lips shape an almost inaudible response. "Not real."

When encouraged to explain, he points to strokes of gray and darker gray on her creation reflecting the last zebra stripes of daylight. "The lines you've drawn here aren't real. And here. They don't exist in the world."

Not real. She could demand the truth but withholds because she knows the statements offered are sincere.

Not real. The truth then? A pounding heart is real enough and true yet its lexicon may not be apprehended, which is closer to what he means to say about her work. He inhabits a quantitative topography reckoned with tape measures, she the realm of imagination. Because she understands what he accepts as real and rejects as not real, and does not feel the need to defend her lines, she can also appreciate why his reaction to the painting fails to recognize her idea of truth no matter how accessible or arcane, yet her skipping beats acknowledge that lackluster discourse in this instance may broaden the rift between them to unbridgeable aspect. She could explain how some lines might suggest physical contour, but others are not to be taken literally and can instead denote qualitative gradation or equality or inequality or a score of other qualities. Could but does not elaborate on the possibilities because the strokes are real to her. She does not clarify why they are genuine to her or what she had intended by them because the marks are simply resident on canvas to speak their language, indeed must "speak" that way, as can words in combination on a page that have no physical referent but are nonetheless true, or phrases suggesting a reality that is untrue, or expressions claiming one thing but meaning the opposite, as does a young woman's racing heart on this occasion.

Metaphor. The figurative. Irony. She might have used those descriptors as well but does not offer them because she lacks sufficient confidence to explain and suspects such terms will carry elusive meanings until her dying day. Because she is convinced most people live and die failing to comprehend them properly though it is possible, she suspects, that much in art and experience – living with or without Mr. Hairy Knuckles – is metaphor and a lesser portion ironic.

Because she is suspicious, fallible, but has enough evidence, she reviews other lines tugging in memory just now. All men are created equal. We live in a democracy. Half-truths to be half believed as though it were straightforward to separate the part that is true from the part untrue and know by what logic and in which context truth or falsehood might be reversed. As though it were reasonable, when precept departs from reality, to value the principle as even more essential and hold to it all the tighter. As though everyone does not cling to fiction for comfort until the grip becomes unmanageable. Fiction about equality, democracy, love.

In the silence accompanying an artist's cerebral explosions, cinematic, one line suggests to her another. A whale swallowed Jonah, and they both lived. Columbus discovered America. Manifest destiny justified the usurpation of native lands. Statements she recalls from childhood during an era when folks embraced myth as fact, but if literal interpretations are discredited by evidence available to all these days then what is true? What is real? That parents persist in being hypocritical, teachers and preachers are disingenuous, radio and TV mislead the public, and books and newspapers print lies while lovers opine. Absurd to think them all myopic.

Preposterous to think so. Nearsighted nonetheless, she knows, her brawny woodworker along with the rest.

As well the more current lines from pundits as if to suggest the propositions they trumpet are either everlastingly true or novel insights for today's world. Corporations decreed to be people by some good old boys wearing robes. Man evolving from apes, touted as defensible ridicule by dogmatists poo-pooing biology. Bungling teachers guaranteed tenure, trickle-down economics sure to work, and a Constitutional right to bear arms sanctified as gospel. Terrorists arising from advocates of a single religion. She is no historian but knows the founding fathers were less than infallible in their advocacy, so our modern-day right to bear arms can be interpreted to include what? Muskets used back in the day? Assault weapons? Laser-guided missiles and nuclear arms? She is reminded of irascible boys with dangerous toys and self-serving ploys inspired by erectile fixations. She is reminded of him. Her lover.

A matter of interpretation then, the political and moral aphorisms about which she dare not speak her mind candidly for fear of preaching, of offending Grandfather or Aunt Shirley or the man sitting nearby, any man, because she knows the claims suggest realities absurd. She does not just suspect it: she is dead certain they are false.

Although she admits to herself it is preposterous. Is. To know with certainty right from wrong about such lofty or mundane propositions when others do not. To know more than others. Her? Yes her. Because she reads Darwin for entertainment. The original *Origin*, the elevating *Descent*. Feels shortchanged in youth upon discovering for herself as an adult that man and apes evolved from a common ancestor, not one from the other as a child believer is told, and then experiences a sense of veneration afforded by one man's breathtaking reasoning. Oh. Yes. That is something quite different. Elevating. She googles gastric pH to sample the digestive waters, wondering if a person could survive inside a whale. Ponders representations of love in poems and cinema and art. Remembers love and yearns for faith but encounters cracks in the texture of both. Fissures. As in metaphor, if that is metaphor. And the rest? Undeniably, empirically erroneous.

Myths advertising higher knowledge but constructed for a cause. A cause not always just, not often just, rarely just. Land of the free. To stand in unemployment lines. Land of sweet liberty where all men are created equal. Except for minorities and women and those other people. Figures of speech, adages, maxims with a purpose, clichés mouthed to keep people in line. Lines designed to keep people sidetracked by proclaiming one thing while implying another. Know the difference or grow up dumb. Grow old in ignorance while nothing changes. Die stupid.

Honest labor is rewarded. Translation: the poor must be lazy, poverty dishonest and deserved. Honesty is the best policy. For whom? Pimps and prostitutes alike? Lovers? Lawyers and politicians? Children more than parents perhaps, or is it the other way around? Is she to include within the oversimplifications car dealers, bankers, and corporate America? And when is honesty best? When buying a vehicle but not selling one; when purchasing stock in a company but not running one; when audited but not preparing one's taxes; when answering vital questions from physicians but not hopeless ones from the demented or doomed. As for the doomed, the meek shall inherit the Earth. Fanciful assurance by the nonmeek to keep the meek meek.

After reading Darwin she devises a rule astonishing

in its simplicity. In seeking answers, ignore talking heads and go to her Galàpagos. As Darwin did. Wondering what poverty means, she volunteers to work in impoverished neighborhood islands. Should all teachers have tenure? She listens to marooned students and rescuing teachers she knows rather than the inept. To discover whether being gay is chosen, she talks to gay acquaintances who laugh at the notion. Homosexuality condemned as choice but heterosexuality exalted as innate? If heterocoupling is righteous and inborn, who but the deranged would choose otherwise? In what world? Planet Schizoid inhabited by a masochistic minority and vainglorious majority worshiping a pantheon that whimsically sanctifies some and vilifies other minions as abomination. Trickle-down wealth. Bolstering what? The minimum wage? She decides that modern controversies are complex, yet solutions are not intractable, so she draws her own lines to convey impressions of truth on canvas.

Oh say, can you see now? She worries she has grown cynical but has evidence she is far from being cynical enough, understands that nothing in her work or about the absurd expressions repeated all her life is black or white, that various shades of gray are of genuine interest. Considers the most ennobling human enterprise to be creativity. So what? What now?

Just for fun. Draw more lines. Go out and dance the night into a happy tantrum while feeling the beat beat. Let painters and dancers and musicians rule the nation.

Enjoy bright sun tomorrow on exhausted shoulders if there is sunshine, or taste the genderless snow descending silently in half-light if there is snow. Hoot despite the burden; laugh with one who knows how to laugh along. Who enjoys living. Loving. Rocks your world. Ooo baby!

She thinks back to mornings when youth held dewy promise, to her lifeline re-envisioned by a dawn's early light when as a girl she walked the rusting tracks that once aimed locomotives from the field behind her house toward a hopeful west. Tracks that followed the straight and narrow for miles before snaking around foothills along a path of least resistance. Her trajectory as well, avoiding the gravitational pull of a grade and paying a toll by never aspiring to high terrain. Measured success on the level, always; expanded vision from the peak, never. Failure to ascend, fearing the descent. Until now.

While they are together today at sundown. Because she has drawn her lines and studied his, knows his by heart. The folds at wrists, crinkles around eyes, furrows on forehead, creases veering into groin, and lines from lips. Especially between the lines from his lips when he means to convey guarded optimism. When he means well. Where she sees the end of a line.

Out of the blue of pre-evening. When he asks why. After he asks how can she know suddenly, finally, and now? She answers with his lines.

"Because your lines are not real." That is her position,

countering his angle of former repose with words he cannot misinterpret. "The lines I see and hear from you don't exist in my world."

★

Observing her posture on the cushions, how she edges to gain distance and lifts herself slightly while speaking. Not about a painting. Responding instead to his lines about her lines, the ones that to her are about him.

It is serious, he realizes. His throat is sand, tongue a broken cord. He struggles to find the language and a voice to express it within a body dispossessed of verbal capacity, to liberate feelings corralled within barriers imposed by external judgment. Seeks to answer her without spending an evening in creative debate, whatever creative debate might mean. Without provoking outrage over reactions sincerely conveyed, making subsequent honesty more difficult. He wants to tell her yet suffers from spiritual laryngitis.

"I love you," he almost hears himself say but is not sentimental and hasn't the voice. "This is not about art or politics, religion or money. This is about two people." But he says nothing. "This is about your work, which I don't understand, and my work, which you do not value." Words felt as stabs in the chest before they are usurped by other thoughts.

Half the daylight hours he worries about what he is

doing. The right thing? Enough? If he had been clear from the beginning, would that have helped? To explain when he first realized that he could never play simultaneous roles of confidante, critic, comrade for a cause. That he came to her with insecurities and burdens. That he enjoys art in his way, casually, and enjoyment must be enough. That he always has and always will attend her art openings despite the social intimidation he feels in crowds – abandonment amid luxury like a child left on an oversize mattress. He will observe and listen without claiming expertise but will never understand the value of art criticism. His nature. His downfall. His saying it: would that help now?

He sees things simply. Admits to weaknesses, failure to be more forthcoming from the start – the alimony and two children – when being candid mattered most. Dwells on what is real. Bills are real, debt is real and termination of service. Sees a balanced budget and mastering one's accounts as evidence of maturity but can't credit using one credit card to pay another. Sees things in black and white and does not want to see red.

He doesn't understand her claim that everything about Wall Street is criminal or her obsession with social justice for farm workers and welfare folks when a person – you, yourself – is suffocating under debt and worried about prospects for the next job or whether there will be another job when a prospective client assesses a damaged hand as unreassuring evidence. Her excuse of artistic temperament to justify avoiding the bottom line, denying red ink and collection notices for nonpayment. Reasoning he cannot fathom.

He is not naïve about democracy and its place in history. He appreciates that the democratic process in Washington might be dead these days or a lie and that real democracy hinges on participation by the people. We the people of course, but how can ordinary men participate when working double shifts? Democracy demands involvement, yes, and he has nothing against tax reform or gay marriage, but must a person step forward to volunteer every time? He feels a misalignment of political interests and disconnected from her bleeding-heart involvement. Arguing over the dinner table whether welfare or warfare is appropriate or inappropriate. Pointless. A rational conversation with her about Palestine? Unlikely. Weekend debates about conservative failings or progressive ideals. To what end?

And the rest of it: silly, occasionally absurd. Violent, she says. Barbaric. Sunday football on TV for the brainless masses. Pagan, his hunting ducks once a season. The only forms of recreation he allows himself all year. Where is the crime?

To change her mind. Impossible.
To chide about money. Foolish.
To explain himself. Hopeless.
Score as a compatible life partner. Fail.

★

In the morning she arranges on the work surface – hers alone to clutter now – oils and brushes, colored pencils and charcoals. She selects what is required for the day and slips the items into a beaded portfolio purchased from a women's cooperative in Tanzania supported by the UN's Independent Labour Organization. In the passenger seat and foot well of a pickup he rummages through four seasons of clothing and extracts sweats and a jacket. A tool belt hugs his hips.

Sunlight catches the beaded surface and returns to her eye a vibrant spectrum from the portfolio. Rays glint from a chrome-plated tool hanging from his belt. Masculine and feminine flashes are temporally coincident and kissing cousins of astronomical proximity but streak through different galaxies. It is a morning much like any other in winter, but clearer than most. It is not the start of day either of them envisioned a year ago or yesterday morning. To lighten the weight of her body, she challenges herself to picture a sweet spring of renewal. He thinks of stretched canvas and knows it has to do with an absence from his life. Later in the day she remembers the empty flat. From this time forward, he imagines, he can manage a budget freely, perhaps begin to save money down the road. As for passion, his saliva thickens. As for love, her eyes water.

Still. When all is said and done she knows he is a good egg. Despite everything, he values her spirit, never mind the blind spots. It is possible for two people to agree they will not engage one another on contentious topics, such as social justice and the meaning of art, is it not? A truce along the lines of Don't Ask, Don't Tell reimagined for a contemporary couple living in the home of the brave. That is possible, yes?

They meet at a coffee house and wonder. He does not believe success likely but would give it a go; she talks about paired friends whose peace accord apparently works well enough. There is the problem of honesty of course. There is the issue of money. There is the certain pleasure of sex, the possibility of love. They venture outside in broad daylight to find the hour advanced – by emotional fallout from polar views – to indigo dusk.

12. TED'S FATHER

As a courtesy to folks unfamiliar with the expression (let's assume a 90% probability of softness in French pronunciation) the phonation is trump **LOY**, and the phrase roughly means fool the eye, the way those sidewalk drawings entice people into thinking there's a bottomless pit ahead when it's just a clever trick of drawing in chalk on a slab of cement. Or maybe painted in pastels or some other medium 15% of the time. I'm no expert, so 15% is ballpark. It might be less: a couple percent or so. Or more.

Anyway, she hires a designer who's supposed to come with a "fabulous pedigree" – whatever that means in the noncanine world of interior design – and the woman comes storming right in through the main rooms of our house with her nose up in the air as if our overstuffed furniture has some kind of flatulence problem. Or maybe she thinks I do. Immediately I know from her altitude this is going to cost me a bundle, way more than the gopher damages. A good five-will-get-you-ten it runs into five figures.

What I don't expect is how she comes nosing up to me out of the blue one afternoon when my wife is out playing cards with her club people. This person measures a good 6 by 2.5 wide; that's more than 12 square feet of woman coming at you ready or not. Waltzes right up in my face with her blouse grazing my shirt and her breath washing over me like a rip tide. Woah there! On a stink scale of zero to ten, this designer person warrants seven plus. Putrescene, they call it. I don't know why I remember something like that, but I do. I must have heard about putrescene from my dentist, and the word stuck to me ever since, the name of the chemical that causes uber-foul breath in some people. It's the kind of thing I don't forget, the kind of person I am. Putrescene. Super descriptive, you might say, although cadaverine is even better at sounding how it means.

Anyway, inside a week flat there's her artwork on my wall. A done deal you couldn't avoid, but really: art? I wouldn't give you two cents.

So I ask her, expecting a viscous comeback, but no. She's slick. "It's subliminal." That's all she argued after I asked; no other justification for a floor-to-ceiling painting of a walk-in closet on our dining room wall. The drawing, measuring 8 feet by 5 feet wide, is of a partially open double door, a big door standing two-thirds open into which a person can just see clutter inside because it's kind of dark in there. Six shelves full of closet stuff, only painted on the wall, painted shirts on painted hangers, lazy underthings sprawling around. On the messy side.

"Really? A bunch of clothes painted on the wall of our dining room?" I asked her that.

"It's subliminal." That's what the artist tells me. Maybe she means subtle. Some people confuse the two. Maybe I misheard?

"The difference is greater than the similarity." That's how my wife reacts. "As with people," she adds. Maybe I misheard?

Is it me, or that I don't know what my wife is talking about half the time any more? Am I so completely bats by now it's time to blow my brains out? Then I remember a bumper sticker I read someplace. *Wag more. Bark less.* So I keep my mouth shut and write a big check for eleven grand for a drawing – well, painting – of a walk-in closet measuring 5 by 8 feet by about a sixteenth of an inch of paint, however thick a coat of paint is. Some closet. Some dining room wall, courtesy of Ms. Subliminal and my wife.

Sometimes my better half thinks the way a Beach Boys melody wanders all over the place. Everything goes along great for eight or ten beats, and you think you know what's what, then – wham! – the unexpected comes out. The tune she's singing shoots way up high in the air and switches key a couple of times, the way an old Beach Boys song does. On the surface it's all even-steven, then her thoughts migrate into something weird until you realize not only that it makes sense – in an alternative universe sort of way – but that what she's doing is interesting. Unexpected. Beauty of an unexpected flavor from my wife I mean. That's when our gopher shows up again. No, really.

My wife swears the gopher tunneling its way through our side yard waits for her to step outside every morning to "stick its tongue out" at her. Her exact four words. The gopher pokes its head out of a hole and taunts her like some teenager with a tongue, my wife says. I tell her the idea is loony: a gopher is too busy taking care of gopher business to pay attention to her and make some human gesture with a tongue. Does a gopher even have a tongue? How would a gopher know that tongue sticking is a human insult? But no, she's convinced the gopher has her in mind, specifically her, and is deliberately making fun when she gets angry at the loss of another exotic plant to the gopher gullet. As if a gopher cares about my wife, I say to my wife in exaggerated irony to get the point across. Or is that sarcasm? Six to one or a half dozen of the other. As if a gopher gives two hoots about her as the centerpiece of its day, but that's the beauty of the thing, you see. In her mind, my wife is the centerpiece of the entire universe and the garden and gopher mentality, of the neighborhood and celestial plane, of the dining room and that trompe l'oeil closet I've come to accept. Well, accept 50%.

So now when I think something is wacko about what she says or plans to do, like hiring a pedigreedy decorator to paint a closet on our wall, honest to gosh, I bite my lip. I can ignore the painted-on closet on the dining room wall by moving my butt over to face a window instead. Nice view out there too. So I give my odds for happiness a good 95% plus, and if the gopher tries anything smart, I'll just turn the other cheek.

13. GENE

He recalled all the years he'd spent puzzling over connections: the mystery of people connections. But what Gene had mostly heard, back in the days before Ted was born, were imperatives.

"Forward. March!"

As a military brat, only once had Gene spent consecutive terms at the same school in a given town. So. Causation? Then again, only rarely had he escaped his father's verbal disfavor.

"Man up, buddy. There's no free lunch here."

Yet there had been moments after the accident when his father softened even as Gene felt his own spirits descend into a dank well of depression. The nurses were kind through the worst of the post-surgical crying jags caused, they explained, by the anesthetic, but it had felt like a chemical reaction when the icy fluorescent lights and antiseptic aroma in the ward induced another bout of tears. And another. His father finally stormed out of the hospital, a behemoth radiating personal gravity.

"You were not raised to be a cry baby about something so trivial."

The doctors disagreed. A broken arm failing to show any evidence of healing for a month was concerning.

After three months, serious. Six? Baffling to medical science.

Home schooling with his mother for the remainder of that year added further gloom seasoned with books. It wasn't the books themselves that brought him down – he enjoyed reading about other worlds – but an idea that the real and immediate world unfolded elsewhere, somewhere not here. Real life was lived by healthy boys shoving one another jovially on playing fields then racing home for dinner when the hour struck amber. Or so Gene imagined. Imagined, because life was happening all around while he sat with a withering arm tucked by his side, missing out on companionship, shared secrets among friends, each day another penalty for having done the inexcusable.

The body eventually healed, leaving his emotional bearing sagging and aloof, his affective half unsocialized absent friendship. If he rarely missed a beat in math or science, human interactions appeared to be weighted by some mystical algorithm with no clear access. How did they manage it, all the others who found it so easy to relate?

As a compulsive observer of effects he chose to observe then, and to pass the hollow hours, Gene redirected attention as a teenager to empirical matters by recording among other things the high and low temperatures daily. From age 14 when he'd invented a shorthand code, and driven by habit for the next 40 years, he specified in a logbook wind speed and predominant direction, cloud types or lack thereof, and amounts of precipitation on a single line – one line per day – every day. Decades later, he'd accumulated a dozen logbooks. He did not record information owing to need; that's not what drove his wife, Shirley, bless her heart, to distraction. He maintained the logs and other records because he liked documenting a perceived sense of order from randomness, and the weather struck him as partly random with a dollop of predictability. So, might he be characterized as surprised that first morning? Even dumbfounded?

Visible by looking in just the right light after an overnight snowfall, the feature might have gone unnoticed except for a sunrise trace of shadow accentuating animal tracks. A rabbit, a bird or two, possibly a fox along with something rare. Adjacent to nature's imprints ran the perplexing.

To render the apparition interpretable while dismissing impossibilities, Gene's subdued dance of discovery initially turned on a central point: interpreting how during the dark hours the line might have come to be carved into eight inches of new snow. A foot of fresh powder on the ground hardly qualified as unusual in mid-January, but an engraved line in the snow?

Others might have reacted differently, but Gene immediately wondered about origins and whether it might be feasible to "read" the line in some manner. Most folks would have dropped the matter after a minute of befuddlement, but maybe "line" was the wrong way to look at things. A better descriptor, Gene considered, might be subsidence, partly in the geologic sense but with a personal twist. Or a meteorological anomaly. Then again, perhaps labels didn't much matter. He was not the type of man to credit palm reading or astrology, convincing himself instead even as a teenager that parlor schemes of that sort were merely deceptive and – like phrenology or any other pseudoscientific hokum – tailored for the credulous disposed to suspend skepticism along with neural activity in a good chunk of the parietal lobe. Neither did he come to a voluntary undertaking such as this one with scientific training, but nevertheless placed considerable faith in logic and deductive reasoning. No, faith was the wrong word as well. Confidence. Gene had confidence that a phenomenon associated with Mother Nature must have a rational explanation. So, too, for the line in his yard even if the same could not be said of human behavior.

Yet in this instance, time alone could help or hinder explanation. Though infrequent during the coldest months, a warm spell was possible. More likely, an additional snow accumulation would obliterate the writing – if it *was* some kind of message expressed in writing – and that would put an end to the business if destructive metamorphism didn't complicate matters first. But let's not jump to conclusions, Gene cautioned himself.

He thought back on how the morning had begun. One step at a time. Before heading into the kitchen to brew a pot of morning coffee on the massive stovetop – a task he was getting the hang of doing on his own – he'd happened to glance out the dining room window that faced due south. From that position, he'd spotted an unexpected shadow running at a 30-degree angle to the south wall of the house, and his gaze locked on the scene. The feature stood out as a stripe on the snow – reminiscent of an illusion of water on a desert road, but no mirage in this instance – a dark streak that appeared exceptional because no trees grew nearby that could cast such a trace, let alone a straight line. No electrical poles or wires and nothing else dropping naturally or unnaturally from overhead could explain the indentation, if that's what it was. From where he paused at the window, returning with coffee in hand, it appeared to be simply a line, straight as far as he could make out, possibly extending a couple of inches down from the top layer and running one hundred feet or more in length.

He set the coffee pot on a low flame before slipping into parka and gloves. After hugging the house under the eves to avoid disturbing the scene, he dropped to his haunches and craned forward, checking first to rule out the likelihood of a practical joke by one of the neighbors' boys, fine kids but given to pre-adolescent pranks. If that were the case, telltale footprints would be visible somewhere along the line, but nothing marked the snow other than adjacent tracks of a few woodland animals.

While on his knees he thought to scoop a gloveful from where he knelt, allowing the powder to sift through fingers while conjuring in his mind's eye what he could recall about natural changes in surface snow over time. He knew quite a bit actually, having lived in the country for a good portion of his adult life, but most of all how complicated the process could be. He understood that the delicate arms of fresh snow crystals easily crumbled to round off what had been flakes into miniature ice balls, just as sifted snow disintegrated now through his fingers. The common observation, that ground snow loses volume and settles into a composition resembling ice grains, was technically called destructive metamorphism. That happened when temperatures did not vary much through the snowpack from top to bottom. Wind, warming sunshine, and direct pressure could also change the crystals, again breaking the arms and sometimes freezing smaller into larger crystals. The result of some of those alterations was a denser material that compacts well and makes great snowballs.

A different set of changes took place when snow accumulated into an insulating layer and temperatures near the ground stayed relatively warm compared to frigid blasts of air above. Then, new crystals could form a loosely packed layer toward the bottom or next to the ground – something called sugar snow – through a process of constructive metamorphism, a development underlying certain avalanches according to the experts. So much for The Science of Snow 101.

Of course avalanches did not occur in a level yard, and constructive or destructive changes hardly entered the equation at the crack of dawn when overnight snowfall remained light and powdery. So much airy powder, reminiscent of – what? In Gene's imagination a vague image materialized, something to do with the blush of youth. Something about young love.

He stood to relieve the pressure on his ankles and conjured his wife – well, soon to be ex-wife if things didn't take a turn as the result of some human metamorphism. Some folks seemed to have the knack for maintaining relationships over the long term, of mutually reinforcing what one spouse could do for the other, providing insulation against adversity or chilling blasts out of the conceptual north, so that both parties prospered in the final analysis, both individuals remained protected, building layers of trust and reinforcing the positive aspects of marriage. Such a relationship ensured warmth down under the skin along with fringe benefits that included a sublimation of kinetic energy into new life. A kind of sugar snow for adults. Offspring.

He and Sheila had managed to get that part right during the early years, locking in financial security along with children who seemed to prematurely develop minds of their own, for better or worse. Increasingly worse in one case.

But after the kids started school, the couple never seemed to recapture the spirit of a partnership, settling instead into variations on themes of self-induced and other-inflicted injury that snowballed over time. Crystals of snow underwent structural damage with time, whereas humans went directly for the heart and soul. So they had known the best in each other and given up the best, and having lost exactly that, was it not dangerous or at the very least unwise to expect a return to what had been? Was it not better to simply walk away from failed love? He'd recently read the opinion of a Nobel laureate on that very subject, a writer celebrated for perception, suggesting it might be advisable not to revisit the past and attempt to disinter a vanquished memory of passion unless one enjoyed being haunted by the irretrievable. Did Gene credit the idea? That it was best to walk away from love? Or to put no stock in love in the first place? The earning of a Nobel Prize spoke to expertise in a given area such as literary brilliance but remained silent as to a laureate's ability to prophesize matters of the heart.

In any event, what had been initially intended by both husband and wife as a honing of uneven edges in a life partner – *just a little off here, maybe a smidgen there* – cloaked in good intentions – *I know you can be a better person if you just ...* – had turned into something unanticipated: emasculation on her part, deprecation on his until the heat of friction degraded what once had been *us* into fragments. Into so much human debris.

Gene stared across his snow-white yard for more than a minute and pictured a firing line. He imagined hearing something heavy dropping to the ground along with a rendering of once-sharp edges into dust. He pictured in his mind's eye well before the boundary of his property the end of the line.

★

Mid-morning, a neighbor phoned asking to borrow a portable generator for some light-duty task out in his barn. With Carl of all people on the phone, Gene hesitated to mention the mystery that had materialized on his own property, yet despite intentions he spilled the beans as he so often did with this particular neighbor. The guy was so personable; who could resist? Within a minute of picking up the receiver he found himself inviting Carl to stop by for a look.

"There he is!" Carl hollered from the driveway after slamming the door of his pickup and poking a mitt in the air in good humor. "So what's that big mystery you got going on over here?"

Gene motioned the neighbor toward the side of the house, both men making their way to the south wall gingerly because of Carl's girth, and pointed across the blanket of white glittering in the sun. The level playing field of the side yard measured about fifty yards wide by sixty deep, interrupted only by the animal tracks. And, of course, a line running more than one hundred feet from house toward a stand of fir trees in the distance. Neither man said a word for several moments as clouds of vapor marked escaping breaths.

Gene found himself anticipating the verbal exchange. As a predictable sort of person, Carl would probably bring up something to do with crop circles or the like. Maybe this was similar to crop circles, he'd suggest, only in winter, or maybe the ground had cracked underneath for some reason. To which Gene would shrug at his neighbor's proposals and say something to the effect: No, Carl, the ground's been frozen solid for a month; you know that. No ground movement going on either. But when Carl did open his mouth to speak, what he suggested had nothing to do with crop circles.

"Maybe there's a pipe running along down there. You know, a pipeline or something?" Carl imbued the remark with the rising inflection of a question, the way teenagers sometimes do, though it was not a question, and Carl was far from being timid when it came to offering opinions.

"I've lived here for twenty years and done a fair share of digging. There's no line, no pipes buried in that area of the yard. No gas or electric and no water or sewer. If there were, we'd have seen this sort of thing in the past after it snows, don't you think?"

"Uh-huh. Maybe so, unless you weren't looking."

The two men stared across the yard as if it might relinquish spontaneously an answer to the puzzle, then once or twice up at the sky until Carl scrunched his mouth sideways. "Darned-ist thing." And that's as far as speculation went until Carl remembered why he'd driven over in the first place and turned to head to the garage to wrestle the portable generator into the bed of his pickup before driving away.

After the racket of the neighbor's vehicle died down, Gene continued to stand before the feature, contemplating how nothing in his field of vision changed on a scale of seconds or minutes. Only if he came back an hour later to stare, or half a day, would the lighting alter, shadows shift, perhaps the texture of the snow degrade a bit as well if temperatures varied from the sun ducking behind some clouds and re-appearing. But the line hardly changed its appearance over the course of a day. Or after a couple of days for that matter.

Three days later, something occurred to Gene that he'd not noticed before. The original animal tracks were clustered on one side of the line. Day after day the same thing seemed to happen: more fresh tracks appeared on one side of the line and remained on that side. Did the critters sense something about crossing a boundary that he could not comprehend? He remembered how Shirley started coming towards him not exactly sideways but with one shoulder first. Her agnostic piety had always bordered on snobbery, and he didn't mind that, in fact rather admired it, but when her posture altered slightly into a half shrug when the two were together, it seemed as though she might be planning to lead with a kiss or punch, and he didn't know which was worse: an interpretation of her advance as amorous or contentious. Why he should recall such details now was not obvious either. A fringe on her forearms, the smell of burnt tea when she became overheated, the way she had of turning away abruptly when she had no idea what something meant – the answer to a question or how to take a joke – and a swerving recovery in contrast to her usual fluid movements. Awkward to observe, yet endearing. A separate species, his wife, like the hares and foxes that visited the property. But charming nonetheless.

Nothing else changed over the short term. The line, the yard, in his life these days.

But the unfolding of a life over the years, decades of a failing relationship with its polishing of jagged edges until a life direction seemed to flicker in retrospect or advance too swiftly to comprehend or redirect: that was different. Too much happening too quickly in uncontrolled directions. No time for closure, then wham! Too much time on hand. All at once, too much closure.

He kept returning to the line at odd hours of the day and night – sometimes just after sunrise or at 2 a.m. in the moonlight when he couldn't sleep – maybe because this latest experience was in such contrast to what he'd known before. The line felt accessible in the physical sense, open to interpretation, neither inviting nor resisting – or rather, a bit of both, testing the credible but defying explanation. A straight line in the snow.

Sometimes while standing over it, he imagined looking down on himself from above and observing the top of his head next to his wife's, two people linked at the hip for a period while engaged in a duet and waltzing around in circles. Walking in circles, talking in circles, noticing details or failing to notice the same details over and over, year in and out, in a rut of least resistance that took a circular course seen clearly only after viewing at a distance. All the while leading back to now, when he found himself at a standstill before a line running straight away into the distance and ending there. Now, thinking there had to be more.

On the sixth day, Gene headed one last time out into the steely half-light just after sunset and pressed his back against the wall of the house to face the yard. He focused on the field of white so that the line appeared discernible, but barely so and increasingly indistinct as the light of day diminished, and his ears caught the patter of a thousand fragile crystal landings from the silent clouds as Grandfather Moss again whiskered a hoary mantle on the yard.

14. TED'S NEPHEW

An aromatic jolt reminiscent of a factory-fresh luxury car gone slightly gamey on the inside tingled his nose. Beyond the entry, layers had been stacked on racks that reached the skylights, and a handful of people roamed the aisles. Those he could see from where he examined a single culatta of buffalo appeared to be rawhide-rugged middle agers, some borderline daft.

"One does not sew."

So cautioned a fleshy female stationed on the opposite side of a discount table, where she fingered a baby-falo. He expected her to waddle in reptilian fashion – elbows jutting, one eye wandering – but she moved with grace. Five earrings through the left ear, a nose ring, and eight black fingernails glinted as she spoke. Her right ear was taking it easy with the doo-dads.

"One stitches... leather. *Stitches*, mind you."

The admonishment came from someone who probably knew about stitches, in response to his remark that working (he'd used the word "sewing") hides was a fairly new interest. Only that much was easy to convey, so he explained nothing more on this amiable Saturday morning while loitering across from a woman in a leather-goods warehouse.

Merchandise piled on either side of the aisle ranged from capra to croc, buttery deerskin to latigo cowhides prepared as splits and sides or half hides up to 9 feet in length. The motives driving his fascination with leatherwork remained as arcane as mysteries surrounding his own childhood. Files on lineage had been sealed, leaving medical histories unknown. That's the story he'd been told. So were his real parents alive or dead, vibrant or frail with heritable afflictions? Had he really been dumped, and what led to his abandonment as a child? Only blurs and burrs populated his skull where other people kept memories of biological family. Height and intelligence were coded in his DNA along with fair skin; maybe a penchant for leatherworking originated there as well?

"Oh, I wouldn't say they were fussy about their selections so much as particular in knowing exactly what they need."

The woman paused to verify he was listening. He registered half of what she said.

"Why, just the other day I saw one of them in here with those horns grafted on her forehead." She pointed to a temple, apparently hoping for a reaction. "Right here under the skin. You know?" The idea of temporal implants seemed to please her.

She had his attention again. "One of them..." apparently referred to the S&M crowd, which Ms. Nose Ring felt inclined to re-introduce into a zigzag conversation that had left the dock on a casual bearing centered on social niceties. Was she trying to shock, the better to assess his character? He eyed the contours within a black leather halter as she reached sideways to stroke a lambskin, flinched at the idea of assessing any female's curvature so blatantly, and yet could not help picturing a waterbed. This woman must have been a rebellious teen as well, dashing off to a city parlor for another piercing or tattoo. As alien as such inclinations were to his temperament, he knew the territory, suspected that if those breasts were to spill from undergarment restraints, they'd ripple a familiar topography and tease a single silver nipple ring against her flesh. But how could he know? What was he thinking? He shook his head.

The woman continued to jabber as he pictured sparsely furnished rooms yielding off an unlit hallway, walls exuding the smell of sweat and old leather. He imagined hearing faux cries of arousal suggesting pain or pleasure or both until her voice yanked him back into the present.

"... just like children," she allowed.

The stranger's tone mellowed as he experienced another image, maybe more like a vision, though he was not one to credit visions. A kitchen filled itself with sunshine to spotlight a rectangular table of mid-century design as a mother attended a child in a highchair set at one corner, spooning baby dabs of yellow goop from a glass jar. Perhaps Ms. Earring had parented this youngster – a boy? A girl? – some decades in the past. Each time the mother dipped the spoon, she touched it to her lips first for a pretend-taste of encouragement. He felt the goop on his own skin but focused on the jar – Banana Puree – just as the image faded to a silver nose ring dead center on his fovea.

"...just like children," the woman was saying. "Sometimes they come to meet and swap addresses at this very spot."

"Who?" He looked around the warehouse and waited.

"Yes, you know, sometimes they playact at being children, sitting in a highchair to be spoon-fed and all that." She sucked air and snickered. "Part of the game, all that leather and metal they wear. Just gamesmanship."

Was this woman privy to images within his head? She'd been whimsical at first, perhaps to win his confidence, but what was she driving at now? If her intent were to dim the house lights, he would wait for the curtain to rise. He couldn't ignore how she would always maneuver the talk back to the leather crowd – her people, her S&Mers – as though she couldn't help herself, talking as a lover talks. A woman in love is compelled to gush about her beloved while telegraphing nonchalance, yet in the present case making a game of her own enjoyment.

He guessed she'd lived in two worlds, something like himself. Only different. Her worlds were straight-laced versus bent, both occupied by the time most individuals settled into family-hood. Perhaps she'd had a strict upbringing and been saddled with a child or two before glimpsing alternative paths, racy and so delicious that she simply must have a taste. How long the escape from convention into risqué territory? One year? Twenty? After she'd satisfied herself with a joyride, only the black calfskin halter-top remained as telltale evidence along with the nose ring, earrings, and fingernails.

People needed something in their lives, he understood. They needed excursions and indulgences, tattoos or piercings, maybe adventures into dungeons or belfries, or family recollections from childhood. People required comforts to relieve tedium and provide a sense of self. People needed guns.

The image of mother and child again charged his thoughts with possibilities ranging from wishful thinking to fact. The vision could represent the parent he'd always wished for, or it might be nothing but false memory. All he knew was he'd stumbled past a threshold of some sort, allowing him to experience sensations in two, simultaneous dimensions and timeframes: the here and now on the one hand, and a suggestion about the past on the other.

"...as I watched what she was picking out, I thought she would gravitate toward the softer material, like this, but no..."

The idea of testing present possibilities sent an electric current down his spine. The woman held out a single bend of cowhide, rubbing it between fingers as if to draw him into the game. With the middle finger of her free hand, she touched some irritation or crumb just to the side of her mouth. He leaned closer as the feeling of familiarity intensified.

"You have to realize certain leather is stretchy, but some of it isn't much at all, depending on thickness. Here, feel this."

In the kitchen, something changed. Light shone as brightly as always, air through the open window came as fresh as an Adriatic breeze, but something appeared to be happening to the baby.

He extended an arm to accept the leather, rubbing it between his fingers to feel a distinct warmth and pliability.

"You see what I mean?" He saw what she meant. "Now if you need to bind someone tightly, you might want a little give, don't you think? Not like upholstery goods or saddlery. You don't want the goods cutting into flesh – unless that's the thing you're after. Ha!"

"Of course." He answered absently, without troubling himself with the implications of what he was saying or what one might be "after."

Qualities more adult than childlike re-formed the flesh of the child in his head as he looked at his own hands. Was this still *his* dream or someone else's? Maybe it was a case of two people having the same dream with shared memories. Who was the child, exactly, and why did it feel so familiar as it aged, as if he could inhabit the skin, slip inside and sense everything *it* sensed? He focused his internal gaze. The mother wore a nose ring glinting in the sun now. Below the ring, something yellow, something moist, adhered to one side of her lip.

The woman's tongue flitted, but did not reach its target.

He knew the chill of saliva on a white handkerchief applied to his cheek, tongue and saliva, then wet rubbing. How did he know? Was this fantasy realism – a fiction so longed for that it assumed the guise of reality to replace reality?

He reached across the table of leather goods toward the place beside the woman's lip –

"Are... are... ?" he stammered.

"Yes, hon?"

"Are you... ?" – as she leaned forward to receive his touch and a shared possibility.

15. LORENZO AND TED

He leaves a note on the pillow after the morning alarm sounds, honoring his vow to practice English each day and be true to his word. When the children are in bed in the evening, she will join him again at the table to review his words and correct mistakes. The note reads:

> *Mamá. You keep papá warm allnight to unser his heart.*
> *Warm now still in the heart. Go to work. El dinero for*
> *milk and sandawitches to kids and Ester eggs color to-*
> *morrow. Come home late. Quiet. Papá tired.*
> *We love again.*
> *Lorenzo*

He releases the door latch to dampen the clatter and scuffs down a sidewalk while listening to murmurs of a city in darkness that admits nothing over the distant rush of iron wheels on tracks, a post-apocalyptic hum muffled by atmospheric humidity. The signature grumbling of a truck's spent muffler grows loud with approach, the racket echoing off houses across the street as the old vehicle rounds an intersection, headlights lending apparent motion to bumps on the asphalt surface, brakes huffing the vehicle to a stop. Three men press shoulders in front while three more doze in the bed of the truck with backs against the rear window wall. He feels the tailgate weight before climbing onto the back for a drive to the site, his collar tight against a traveling wind. Six passengers shift sideways with the twists and turns, silently nodding an early hour into dawn.

★

The phone rings three, four times — more some evenings — causing Ted to wonder if his registration on the National Do Not Call Registry has lapsed. He finds handwritten notes from a previous year and Googles the website to learn that a one-time signup is all that is necessary. Registration does not expire.

The phone rings again. Duped by anticipation of some emergency: how many times? Could it be his aging father on the line again, or their daughter calling from New York, or... something worse? But the giving in and pickup is followed by dead seconds on the line, total giveaway for solicitation invariably reaching a peak of intrusion at mealtime. Fire departments collecting for families of heroes killed in action, brave men with children. We must remember them, no? Police organizations sponsoring benefits for hospitalized tots, hairless following treatment. Staggering statistics. Is he aware that somewhere between 12 and 20 percent — maybe more — of the world's population does not have clean water or basic sanitation?

Does he appreciate that 2 billion people have no access to electricity? Third-world hunger, mutilated women someplace in Africa, victims of rape, fanaticism, ignorance. Countless ruined lives and the living hell of political refugees stumbling across borders. Shaking women and children. Naked. Tortured political prisoners and unconscionable suffering. Overwhelming. Everywhere.

Nor is it only "over there." Homeless souls wander the streets of Ted's otherwise prosperous city, many off their meds, some insane and reeking of secretions or expiring from heat or cold, dependent on handouts. Impossible to fathom. Have-not's doomed to doorways and concrete slabs in urban centers around the country, bad enough; then again, the have's, in some ways, worse. Their unrelenting pleas on the phone or at the front door. Scouts with ruddy cheeks gathering food (even a can of something will help, Sir); girls in pressed uniforms with 26 kinds of cookies; cherubic neighborhood children peddling school raffles to pay for classroom computers, magazine subscriptions to underwrite field trips, hopeful faces looking up.

A country in shambles from sweet deals orchestrated by fat suits from megacorporations exchanging cash for favors. Corruption at historic levels locally, evoking a chorus of sighs among the neighbors gathered at backyard barbecues. What if no one took action in a democracy, they ask. What might happen if a million people marched again for social justice? People with petitions, yearning to the do right thing. You know in your heart...

Yes. Ted knew in his heart.

Political activism offering hope for the hopeful – or at least an alternative to doing nothing. Worthy or otherwise? How could it be unworthy? To join a group of citizens taking to the streets in frustration. Well-meaning people. Or were they simply naïve to the point of blindness, isolated from reality and power brokers by their own hyper-suspicious natures; as opinionated, uninformed, and biased as the opponents they finger as extreme; as susceptible to corruption of moral standards as the blatantly corrupt?

Good intentions rendered into positive change through activism? In what universe can impotence compete with billion-dollar coffers, and what might constitute the motive for trying, Ted asks himself those questions. Conscience? Guilt? Hope? To chant or carry signs. Ridiculous, maybe. Or not. To mingle with the self-righteous, the strident and pretentious. Abhorrent. To invite confrontation with lunatics drawn to hyper-charged political gatherings?

Better to focus on immediate concerns then. One's family for example. One's health. Retirement accounts.

Ted tells his wife and every other family member who happens to be present during the evening meal. Ignore all phone calls, please, between 5 and 9 p.m. Do not pick up the phone. Don't respond to the doorbell. Just don't. Just stop.

One thing at a time, he decides, focus on one thing. Yet the tug to do something. To do one good thing.

★

Two parking lots service the massive home-improvement center, each stretching for a block along the commercial street. The main entrance is designed for access to a customer service counter and returns desk; a second entrance and checkout area is located near the garden department. A bell-shaped distribution of men wearing workpants is stationed along the curb, clusters of four or five men standing their posts at the more desirable locations. For a quarter mile in both directions smaller groups of men form, or individuals stand alone, most middle-aged but a few too weak or too old for a day's hard labor. So many gathered already, he notices, except for the less-used exit.

The truck in which Lorenzo rides stops at the quieter exit. The last three men jump from the bed of the pickup, and Lorenzo follows them.

He waits. He knows he might have to stand much of the day, as he did yesterday. He hopes it will be a good day, a better day than yesterday. He studies secretly each face behind a steering wheel when a car or SUV pulls into the parking lot. Passenger vehicles offer better prospects, he understands, because the pickups are often owned or operated by contractors with licensed help. Skilled labor. The competition. He stands at noon and eats lunch with the other men, sharing water from a 5-gallon plastic container. Maybe today will be better than yesterday.

★

Exiting the drug store, Ted pats his shirt pocket and retrieves the note from Lavinia. As always, the writing is in her beautiful script.

Ted, Don't forget to stop by the home improvement store to pick up two of their large Easter lilies for the weekend. The large ones are on sale today for a good price.

★

A Mercedes-Benz ML350 cruises the lots in search of a parking spot, but nothing is open near the main entrance to the improvement center. At the exit most distant from the garden center, the SUV passes a group of three men before pulling out of the lot. The vehicle returns a minute later and pulls to a stop close to the men. At the curb, the men stop talking and face the car. Through a partly opened window, they hear strains of music – a classical baroque invention – and see a blue glow from the navigation screen and imagine they can detect a faint scent of leather seats.

Hope rises in Lorenzo's chest, rises for his daughter and son though he dare not hope too much or move too quickly. He fights an urge to step in front of the others, thinking: me. Pick me. Because of decency, which prevails, he does not move. The driver must choose.

The dark SUV remains stationary as the window is lowered. Until the shortest of the day laborers takes a step forward.

"Work, señor?"

The man in the vehicle shakes his head. No. Still, the car remains in place. The driver gestures with a roll of the wrist. On the wrist is a fine watch.

Again, from the shortest man. "Work señor?"

Ted answers. "Sorry men, no work today," yet the Mercedes remains motionless. The engine idles as the short man backs off. In response to more emphatic beckoning from the driver, the three men huddle, uncertain, and look away.

Ted opens the door and steps onto the pavement while the engine continues to purr. From a pocket of his sports coat of imported tweed he withdraws something.

The thought of one thing. One thing at a time; one arbitrary act of humanity. Here. Now.

Ted rolls his wrist to beckon the men who still do not move. From his wallet he takes out several bills and approaches the men. Their faces are expressionless as he tucks two bills into a shirt pocket of each man, their eyes on the pavement as if this person were issuing traffic citations or orders for deportation.

"For Easter." This is what Ted says to Lorenzo before returning to the vehicle and driving away in search of a decent parking spot.

★

At dusk, he asks the truck driver to drop him at the Food-4Less rather than his customary store that stocks ethnic items. Before entering the grocery, he examines the two bills unfolded from a handkerchief tucked in a trouser pocket, remembering it is Easter tomorrow. Remembering that ten dollars for each of the children is needed for school next week, as his wife has explained. He has two twenties from today, three dollars in bills from before, and almost a dollar in coins. Inside the market and adjacent to the meat counter, a chiller bin is piled high with hams that have been vacuum-sealed in plastic wrappers. Virginia hams are twice the price. He moves to the hams on markdown today at $1.39 per pound. A good price. A sign announces that if more than $25 is spent on groceries, the special ham is further reduced to half price. Lorenzo tries to figure in his head while taking a ham and moving to the dairy section. If he purchases a half gallon of milk, the bill comes to $23.65. The milk will not last two days, but he has the ham, and the children will each have ten dollars for school.

He stands in a checkout line where customers in front unload packed carts. He calculates again in his head to be sure of his purchases as his turn comes at the cash register. After the children's needs are met, he can spend no more. The cashier, a tall man wearing a white apron, scans the two items. Ham. Milk for the children.

"If you spend 25 dollars today, your ham is half price," the cashier explains.

Lorenzo shakes his head. No señor. He hands this man the money. No more. Still, the cashier wants something of him and uses the public address microphone to call a name.

Lorenzo freezes. He shifts weight from one foot to the other, then back to the first foot, wondering if he should leave. Run. Now. He shifts again while the cashier waits. Something is wrong. He has done something wrong. What? He wants to say something to the cashier, but the man holds up a finger. One finger. Wait.

The cashier speaks to a runner. "Bring me – " But Lorenzo cannot make out the English words that are spoken so quickly.

Again he tries to speak. To explain to the man that he has the money, here it is in his hand, but he cannot pay for more, yet the cashier holds a finger to his lips again. People in line are aggravated. A man next in line makes a show of resting one tennis shoe on a rung of the shopping cart, arching his back into a curve, and moving his head while staring up into space through brown eyebrows. When this man glances around to a woman standing behind him, Lorenzo thinks he hears a sigh from one or the other person. He thinks he hears a growl and detects a shaking head. He thinks he hears a phrase. "Some people." He thinks he sees a rolling of eyes and police in blue shirts coming toward him. Their hair and skin are different from his own – lighter in texture, smoother in character or rougher – and they are impatient, getting angrier by the minute because all contrasts in life are black and white, white and black, and the person holding up the line is a subspecies of their own.

The runner returns to the checkout area with a half gallon of milk, and the cashier scans the second container. Lorenzo stares at the screen showing the purchase amount. It does not increase, but drops by so many dollars. The checker counts change and hands back to Lorenzo nine single bills and six coins. The two men – the checker and customer – look at one another, saying nothing. Everything.

I am a man. You are a man. We do what we can.

Lorenzo returns to the aisles for eggs, beans, and vegetables. He adds a paper container with six coloring tablets for eggs. He stands a second time in the checkout line.

Afterward, he walks home in the cool air. The two paper bags he carries are heavy. At the stoop he sets the bags on the concrete to turn the key as his two children push on the door to dash out and grab his knees. His wife waits for the children to finish and then holds her husband's face with both palms. The question is in her eyes. Work? The answer is in his eyes. No work.

She sees his arms are empty then notices the bags on the cement. She bends down to look inside. A ham. Two jugs of milk. Eggs. Beans. Vegetables. A small paper container with coloring tablets for eggs. For the children. For Easter. Her eyes go up.

Lorenzo starts to say something to his wife. "Today..." but he hesitates, not knowing how to express the thought in English but trying anyway "... we have everything."

Each day, he returns to the parking lot with a note written in good grammar by his wife folded inside a shirt pocket. Each day he looks for the Mercedes-Benz and driver wearing a tweed jacket. He will hand the note to the man and say nothing. Better to say nothing than pretend always to know black from white or white from black.

16. UNCLE SID

You know, I was born 15 years after they said I was. Like I say, that, or else I was born when they said but frozen for 15 years then thawed like a turkey the way they do in those science fiction movies. I should know because I was there. Not at the movies. I mean when I was born, not where I am now. Wait. Where was I?

Oh yes, the odds are stacked against a person being thawed – who believes movies like that? – so it stands to reason I'm 15 years younger. How else do you explain I look 15 years younger than I supposedly am other than to say I am 15 years younger than they say I am? Minus 15 is what it is.

Stand in front of a mirror like you do to shave your face when you're shaving, a young face I might add, and look directly at the nonwrinkles where they should be by now. That's more money in the bank as far as I'm concerned. Nickel for each side of my mouth regardless of smiling in the mirror or not smiling. Cheeks smooth as a billiard ball, so that's a dime. Not a line on the forehead, add a dollar. Upper eyelids without a droopy crease, throw in a fiver for that. Times two for the two eyes. Ten bucks for the nonchicken jowls. Twenty at least for places under the eyes where old people get bags. So that right there is — what? — a couple hundred bucks. I am wealthy I tell you, not some mummyneck. Healthy, wealthy, and wrinkle-free. Take it to the bank.

Anyway, Sarah is always on me not to change my birth certificate, which is what I intend to do as soon as I can get to it. She says not to change the date because I wouldn't get my Social Security checks until 15 years later than if I didn't change the date to the real one. What kind of sense does that make I won't even bother explaining.

Another thing. Every single time I had a car accident, she's the one who's yacking at me do this, don't do this, watch out for that kid over there. Yack, yack, yack. So naturally I don't have a driver's license to get to work that she forgets to set the alarm for anyway back when I worked. Or make my sandwiches. Your mother would turn over in her grave. Did I mention how scattered she's become? I fear she's got a tuber.

Same type of thing with the chainsaw when I was out to the woods doing some cutting she was always on my back about for the fireplace. It's cold in here, it's cold in here, so I go out to the woods to get her off my back. Come quick I yell, but do you think she could find the fingers even after I point where I was pointing? No, of course not, me bleeding like a banshee all the way to the emergency, which I could not drive to myself because I don't have a license to get there and now the left fingers so Sarah had to drive without the fingers for them to sew back the way they can these days. They use ice or something like in the movies.

Or when I got that concussion from the motorcycle thing after her yelling at me all the time you'll crack your skull open, you'll crack your skull open. A person keeps talking about an accident and killing someone no matter how careful you are, sooner or later sure enough it's bound to happen so just don't say it in the first place. Don't say you'll shoot your eye out like they told that little kid with the BB gun before he did in that movie. Well almost did. Or how you're going to hurt somebody on your motorcycle, which is how I ended up like this.

People keep warning I should stop poking fun at the guards because they have these insecurity issues and all and maybe that's so, but I always say life's not worth two hoots if you can't have some fun now and then, which is why I like scotch so much and fast motorcycles and guns. What kind of security is it anyway when the security guys have insecurity about the security they're paid to do? What kind of logic is that?

You can count the evidence on my fingers like a lawyer. Finger one, Sarah denies I am 15 years younger. That's denial. Two, she forgets where I put things like when she wouldn't go to help me get that FBI job like I said I would go to interview, didn't I? Good money too so whose fault is that? Three, she truly believes they will not give me my Social Security for 15 years after it's due.

That's nuts. Which is why I have those big old bags under my eyes now I guess. Four, she's getting fat.

I'm not saying she has a brain tuber because I'm not the expert here, but when you put it all together – the denial of my 15 years and her fat and forgetting and repeating stuff about accidents and breaking my skull – then what you've got is finger five as clear as the nose on your face in a mirror. I don't know if it's what they call haywire from the tuber exactly, but I'm taking her in for an exam first chance I get. When I get out. Six, that's exactly why I'm filing for the quarantine or what you call it, commitment I guess, when I get out. So don't forget to bring her quarantine papers to show at my parole to the parole people like you promised you would. Thanks. Your uncle Sid.

Oh and some quarters for the candy bars I like if it's not too much to ask. They only take quarters after someone new here passed some bills. If you know what I mean.

17. TED'S NEPHEW

In the dark. Not nighttime dark but soul dark.

He opens, then closes his eyes once again – one, two, three times – knowing there will be no difference, wide open or shut: the outside world and retina agree. Both are blank. His body might be levitating from the ground a few inches then settling back down, but there is no up or down here, no way to verify direction. Or swelling. Prone for an hour, his body might be expanding to the size of a truck or stadium; how could he know? If his physical form were collapsing into itself – a sensation he experienced not five minutes ago – he would have no way to verify the change.

It is difficult to breathe. His hands tremble, which is to say he thinks his hands are shaking. It is impossible to make sense of movement or its absence because he can't see his hands in front of eyes. Because the fingers feel cold and unsteady, he grips the edge of the sleeping bag and adjusts some fabric to verify that the digits remain functional. The material rustles as something occurs to him. The dead quiet all around. The unnatural silence. Not a hint of air or whisper in trees from the movement of air through pine needles. Instead, nothing at all. A nothingness so complete in the sound department that a person might imagine it possible to hear the Earth moving through space as it orbits the Sun.

"Wait a minute," he says aloud, startling himself with his own voice. If the earth travels through space around the sun like everybody says, then how come everyone can't hear the sound of that movement? It's got to be a huge and constant thing, as big as sound can get. He frowns and holds his breath, or supposes he is frowning, then relaxes the forehead muscles a bit. Because it is space after all, empty space, and sound cannot travel in a vacuum. Wasn't that true? Still, he listens for a trace of whiplash while continuing to hold his breath, imagining what the earth-sound would sound like and knowing that if it were possible to hear it anywhere on the surface of the earth, it would be here, in this place. But in fact? He hears nothing.

He remembers camping with the family once as a kid. He pictures open skies and a large body of water off somewhere with other kids shouting in the distance, when he hears something foreign. Hears it not in memory, but right now. For real. It comes from nowhere and everywhere at the same time. His head rotates to localize a direction, but the disturbance will not be localized even as its intensity increases, a rushing noise coming from all directions. The trembling of his hands increases as the disturbance draws him out of himself. Then it dawns on him. His heart. It is the sound of his own heart pushing blood around with such force that paying attention only increases the pounding. He tries to concentrate on something outside his body to slow the heart rate, trusting in the likelihood that there is nothing to fear close by. No wise guys out there after his wallet or mountain lions smelling his ass in the neighborhood or from far away for that matter. When is the last time anyone heard of a bear eating somebody for lunch, unless it was in a Western? Not in this lifetime. Except in that 60s book. What was it called? Something about the night of the grizzly. He sighs. Thinks the rhythm of his beating heart might be settling down some. Knows there is nothing out there for miles in any direction except his own skin and a breathing, beating heart, but the knowledge is unconvincing in a night that is just getting a jumpstart on darkness.

Think of something else then. Anything. School even. That time in a seminar with that nerdy professor talking about David Hume or something. The Scottish philosopher who said all kinds of things nobody could understand, but one statement he would always remember. *A man's life is of no more importance to the universe than an oyster.* True enough. True right now. An oyster fretting about – what? Nonsense. The darkness of the dark. The beating of a heart.

An oyster in the wilderness. The thought reminds him of a quote from that Russian he heard once: *If a pistol appears in a story, eventually it's got to be fired.* The idea is not especially deep but rings true maybe because it comes from a big-time storyteller, according to all the experts.

Maybe the best story writer of all time. An important idea perhaps, but is it correct? Must a pistol be fired, and what does it mean if a pistol appears in a story and is never fired? Could that be even more important in a metaphysical sense? Anyone can fire a gun for a hundred different reasons. Fear. Stupidity. Revenge. But what if the predictable never comes about? Maybe that is more profound in terms of morality: a story in which a gun is around but not fired.

He moves an arm slightly to the right, searching, as if someone else might be watching for movement. He feels the object contact a finger and senses the cold. Takes comfort in knowing that the one thing on this Earth that means control is right next to his hand. The thing that gives power over light and heat and life and death is inches from his grip. It is easy to love this power, to want to use it and never give it up. More difficult to let go, and why should he? There is only one fact during the darkness that keeps coming back in his thoughts to lend a measure of satisfaction, like an insurance policy.

He feels the weight of the darkness pressing on his body, flattening the stomach, crushing throat and scrotum, squashing his brain. He wants to cry out but dares not make a sound until a voice says the words. "I never wanted it." Not a voice exactly. His thoughts projected into the openness around him. "I never wanted it to be like this."

This. The way everyone reacts. Which has nothing to do with David Hume or philosophy or Chekov. This. The real. The concrete, here and now and prospect for a future.

His attention, so divided between worlds within and without, begins to lapse as if a human being were a time capsule or a pill dissolving in water. In the dissolution, he feels himself not coming apart but restructuring and fortified by imperfect consciousness, an unfocussed but familiar self-awareness, a more relaxed state of mind and body until consciousness erodes as he slips into a mid-world halfway between wakefulness and dreaming, drifting into and out of sleep granted by the familiar and reassuring presence of cold, hard metal against skin.

PART THREE

18. TED'S FAMILY

Rain the last quarter hour become snow falling gently in gently failing light yet light enough to grace a seasonal harvest with nature's incandescence. They enter by twos and threes to shake frosty crystals from hats and shoulders in the foyer before migrating to living spaces or joining conversational knots around a kitchen island, to catch up and joke while the boys follow a football game on the flat screen and at least one guest finds the bathroom. No one gives the upstairs a thought. Why would they? The relatives – extended family along with two invited neighbors who are childless and just as well might *be* family – wear Sunday clothes and shoot for good behavior this afternoon, though not a Sunday, before second and third glasses of wine liberate tongues.

Holding his bourbon, straight, and surveying the domestic scene, Ted reflects. There is for each of us the world of our imagination and the world as it is. The first, a reality conjured and inhabited by each person as an individual, fallible, interpreted from within but mostly from without according to others, pundits and opinion-makers whose conclusions are notorious. Worse: suspect. The second is the world revealed empirically by science and mathematics. Two worlds. One can live always in the former sphere, as almost everyone chooses to do, or see what actually *is* and experience the latter. As almost no one does. As Ted tries to do now while giving nothing away to Uncle Sid who has hijacked his ear and aims to take it for a spin over a tale about the voluptuous nurse's aide on his ward and her scandalous miniskirt even as Ted maneuvers to break away. But gently. Because Sid has been given permission after many years in lockup to spend this afternoon with the family as long as he is under direct supervision of a responsible person – namely Ted. A highly responsible person, all would agree. Just for a single afternoon, understand. As a test of the man's behavioral self-control on this Thanksgiving Day.

Lavinia checks that the womenfolk have delivered decanters of Chablis and Pinot to the table before announcing dinner in a voice cheerful as the chatter around her. What follows is the always-awkward beat of men standing a moment too long in place, holding chair-backs while the women settle. Ted's father as patriarch picks up the knife to carve a giant, perfectly cooked, golden-brown bird and pass plates down the ranks after each person specifies the desired cut and portion. Wife and Lavinia on his immediate right both request a small serving of white meat, Lavinia's daughter a wing. Ted's first son likes a thick slice of breast, thank you, and so on for the younger son, his girlfriend, then the favorite and favored neighbors from cater-corner down the street. And so on down the opposite side of the table for Lavinia's aunt, Ted's brother Gene and his wife Shirley, Ted's crazy Uncle Sid and frowning Aunt Sarah, then finally for Ted himself seated at the foot of the table.

Before the first mouthful of food or taste of wine is sipped from crystal goblets, Sid asks his nephew the question. "Is Harley here?" Asks the question a second time too loudly. "Where's Harley?"

Ted gives the indirect approach a go, expecting failure. "Not this year, I'm afraid."

"Good old Harley. Why not?"

"Hush now!" Wife Sarah warns.

"Just asking why isn't Harley here, can't I ask?"

Sarah knits her spidery brows as Ted leans sideways before her bosom to avoid answering in a volume that others can overhear. "You wrecked Harley, Sid. Remember. Think back."

"Wrecked Harley. *Me?*" The old man scratches his chin, unshaven for a few days.

"You totaled Harley in the accident some years back." Decades ago Ted means.

Sid is crestfallen as Sarah places a fork in his hand and motions plate-ward. "Hush now and eat your dinner."

Friends and family slice white or dark meat on the best dinner service from Lavinia's pantry, patting lips with linen, kibbitzing, most going for seconds before pies – plural – and bowls of clotted cream make the scene, at which point Ted scoots his chair back and stands to offer his annual postprandial speech.

"My dear family and trusted friends..."

And so on, about the holiday occasion and good fortune of a family whose members are blessed in so many ways. Thinking as he speaks: This is my life. Saying how wonderful it is to have Uncle Sid back at the dinner table after so many years but thinking about the imperfection of humanity – relatives atop the list – and appeal that character flaws can elicit because they draw you in and pull at the conscience and ultimately tell you something about yourself. Perhaps. How people are drawn as strongly by flaws as by strengths in others because the defects so often feel like extensions of yourself.

"What'd he say?" Ted's father asks, cupping his hand midway through the oration.

"He says you ought to pay more attention," snips his wife. And so he tries.

Folks disperse around the house after dinner, members of the gentler sex tackling kitchen cleanup and guys patting stomachs in the living room. On his way to the master bedroom upstairs to fetch a letter from his daughter containing a photograph Lavinia wants to hand around – the snapshot of a daughter's latest and best painting to a mother's eyes – Ted passes the spare room used for storage since move-in day decades past. He stops at the threshold to verify he is not imagining a rustling noise coming from within, when a whimper emanates from the room neither he nor his wife has entered in months. A guest perhaps, or pair of young ones up to something.

Should he investigate? Opting for diplomacy, he stands inches from the door and calls out quietly. "Is someone in there?" He waits. Speaks again after a few seconds: "Hello, is everything alright?"

He is prepared to shrug it off when a yelp comes from behind the door. Ted grips the doorknob and rotates it while shoving the side panel that he remembers sticks tight to its jamb. A second shove reveals a scene at once familiar and alien. Boxes and junk, as he vaguely remembers leaving them, are scattered around the room. Old clothing and children's apparel outgrown and intended for charity spill from shelves and are draped from hooks. All is as expected for the remainder of the room, undisturbed except for the center area where a single taper candle burns. And this. Half in shadow and crouching on what appears to be a cardboard box is his nephew. Trembling. Or apparently trembling on what might or might not be a box, for the lighting is too dim to make out much detail.

"Sir!"

It is a word Ted has never heard this nephew say. A salutation that reminds Ted of James Joyce for some reason he cannot fathom. "Sir!" apparently addressed to Ted himself. As a plea? No, a protest, demand, prayer all in one as his nephew – absent the hometown scene for more than a year without a word to anyone – cowers on the box or whatever it is and appears about to clutch his uncle's ankles as Ted dances back.

"You!" Ted is at a loss. "How did you – " But this is the wrong question, Ted knows, having no relation to what he means to ask his nephew or wants to say. Why here? Why now? Like this? "Where have you been?"

Eyes adapting to the near-darkness, Ted focuses on the box – crate? – more intently, deciding that it is neither cardboard nor crate but what appears to be a child's coffin. Along with something on top that is tied into what looks like a noose, the free end dangling. The coffin is unfinished pine boards, measuring no more than four feet in length, with six uncurved sides.

"What are you... doing here?"

His nephew would clutch his uncle's ankles again save for deft maneuvering on Ted's part as he backs toward the door and grabs the knob. He is almost out the door when he notices a book on the floor – a Bible? – and centered on the volume, a handgun. The candle flickers in a draft and goes out, leaving the room in darkness. Ted scrambles into the hallway and pushes the door shut, pushes too forcefully, causing it to slam. His mouth is agape, through he cannot recall parting his lips. All is quiet in the upstairs hall. He cocks his head and hears only the pings of glasses being rinsed by hand in the kitchen sink – by hand because they are crystal with gold rims – and intermittent laughter from the first floor. He blinks. Considers reopening the door then thinks better and returns to the main floor without the photograph Lavinia has asked him to retrieve.

At the bottom of the stairs he runs into his brother. Ted jerks his head upward and tells him. "Your son is up there."

Gene's face goes blank before sidestepping into a smirk. "Oh yes – ? And what am I supposed to do about that? What would you have me do?"

"With a gun."

Gene takes a step back as if to reconsider. "He's 30 years old, Ted. How do you make a 30-year-old see reason?"

Ted is desperate for another drink but does not answer his brother's question or move away. He waits for Gene to say or do something more.

"If someone has a gun – well…" Gene hesitates. "What can Shirley or I do about it? It's none of my business. Our business. At what point does it become our business, or yours?"

Ted thinks but does not say what he feels. When it's loaded perhaps. Cocked and aimed? Or do you wait until the person is behaving so erratically that you can no longer ignore the behavior? Do you wait until you're looking down the barrel? He pushes past his brother and heads for the bar to fix himself a drink.

Later that evening, when the two boys are out to a movie and Ted's parents are rumbling the rafters of the guest bedroom with snores, the couple has the house to themselves.

Lavinia brushes his cheek with the back of her hand

before pressing lips against Ted's forehead, a tender gesture he welcomes. The afternoon and evening have been a success, they agree, sans harsh words from any quarter. Ted does not mention the second-floor encounter, preferring to think it was his imagination playing tricks. He does not bring up his own doubt or his brother's response. He thinks instead about money. White powder. Violence. His daughter. When Lavinia retires to the bathroom, he tiptoes to the spare room and listens for a moment just outside the closed door. He acknowledges the silence. He refrains from peeking inside because he knows he will find nothing there. No nephew. No Bible or gun, the room undisturbed, as if it had never been occupied, or occupied by ghosts. Ted decides, uncharacteristically, to leave suspicions behind for now together with conjecture and the possibility of ghosts. At least for tonight.

★

It's not as if anyone would deliberately set fire to the house. Would they? *Why* would they?

The dispatcher officially logs the call from a next-door neighbor on Maygrove Street at 2:12 a.m. Orange flames and smoke blossom from a second-story window on the south side of Ted's house, the aspect that faces the next-door couple who are awakened by the stink of scorched siding and play of light on their bedroom ceiling.

Hours later, Ted's brother stands in shirtsleeves on

the curb, shaking his head, tired from driving, vaguely aware of folks up and down the street who are watching the mopping-up operation. Ted's two teenage sons stand a few yards away with smartphones in hand illuminating their sleep-deprived faces during this last hour before daybreak, thumbing keyboards, texting – whom, at this hour? – with updates. Damage, of course, is obvious at the south end of the second story but nothing beyond the repairable according to the fire chief who explains to the homeowner that one response unit will remain on-scene during the morning to ensure there are no flare-ups, as Ted nods acknowledgement and murmurs gratitude over tax dollars in action and local heroes who risk soft flesh to save somebody else's hard real estate. He shakes the chief's hand.

Then the talk of spirits. His brother starting it by whispering. "He's a damned phantom."

Spirit. Ghoul. Sociopath. Ted knows what his brother means and disagrees completely. He and his brother never, during their years together growing up or as adults, have talked about faith, never once as kids, and they do not now, this chilly pre-sunrise hour. There is no reason to debate because they both know it all boils down to only a few things: Gene does not challenge the old childhood – or life – myths. He has no reason to do so; why rock the boat? What good can it do to stir up things that don't matter? Right or wrong, what does it really matter if Darwin is right, or not; or Nietzsche or the local priest or witch doctor; or if things go bump in the night of their own accord, or not; if democrats have a monopoly on truth, or republicans, or progressives, or no one at all? You get up each day and go to work just the same and pay the mortgage. That's what it is, as far as brother Gene is concerned. That's it in a nutshell, except when you worry about the marriage or your offspring and resort to words you don't really believe in because you don't understand.

Deranged. Phantom. Seer. More balderdash. People use such words, not really knowing what they mean because they don't know what else to say.

Another thing Ted cannot abide. The idea of a nutshell. The idea of anything in a nutshell, as if ideas or values can be cooked into submission or distilled before being dumped into smug packages for final comprehension. Too smug by a long shot.

The police file a report after a forensic investigation is done. Probable cause: an unattended candle in an upstairs room. No accelerant has been detected, and there is no evidence of a break-in: therefore, not arson. Definitely not that. Be more careful during the holiday season, Mr. and Mrs. Homeowner. Amen.

"He's turned into a phantom," brother Gene says again about Ted's nephew as the brothers stand together there on the curb while wisps of steam curl from the eaves. A victim does he mean? Brainwashed? Terrorist? Ted buys none of it. All nonsense and far too simplistic. As well, something about the unexamined life he cannot get out of his head.

The general feeling in the family about the matter is that the fire was an accident, a scary nuisance more than anything else. Nothing serious, thank goodness for that, and everyone is inclined to believe it. Almost.

Yet within a few days, several busy-body acquaintances who talk to the family, or about the family, swear they know the lowdown: that the fire was arson and a "street person" was responsible for setting the blaze though such assertions are impossible to verify *ex post facto* because shortly after the "incident on Maywood Street" the annex of the local police department building housing records burns to its cement foundation, and along with it, an affidavit by a "vagrant" who was interrogated for several hours before being released. Someone spotted him in the neighborhood that night, it is claimed. A rough looking sort, probably an "illegal" hauled in for questioning then released. Probably not a Christian. Certainly not that. And Lavinia is said to have mentioned to her women friends something about faulty electrical wiring in a closet upstairs. Possibly. This confession is believed to have been tossed out over nervous laughter and a hastily raised glass of white wine immediately drained of its contents. No mention is made of the dusting of something around one of Lavinia's nostrils or the possibility that Lavinia might have been developing a cold.

Ted does not comment further on the matter. He reflects privately on the tendency to overestimate effects (good or bad) of almost any event or circumstance today on something tomorrow. He recalls that that idea, said to be gaining popularity, is called "impact bias" and thinks it a twenty-first century concept – at least the bias part – but wonders if the actual tendency is not *underestimation* of consequences rather than its opposite. Or can things come about from nowhere at all? With no lasting effects or consequences. No, Ted cannot bring himself to believe such a thing. There are always effects. Causes.

In the middle of the night – a Sunday night before Christmas Eve – he awakens with a phrase buzzing in his head, a phrase weighted with unspecified significance. Or perhaps it is emotional significance Ted senses in the black hours, about himself, or something he was about to say in a dream or has recently thought while awake.

He sprinkled the words.

He hears the sound of those four words as if someone has spoken the odd turn of phrase aloud, suggesting that words are sometimes tossed out like breadcrumbs before pigeons, flung out for the benefit of anyone willing to listen or take them in. Or to not take them in. Words having to do with what is possible or barely possible. Tolerance of individual differences for example. Accommodation to the realities of climate change and ending hunger and understanding the motivation of those people we care about. The incomprehensibility of those who seem not to care. Acknowledgement of greed where greed takes center stage and misery when misery abides. But what words, exactly, are "sprinkled" in this way? Sparingly. And about whom? What are the words?

In the blur of a meta-wakeful suggestion that insight can be derived from a few sprinkled words — the truth about his nephew's motivations for example, or his wife's white-powder habit or man's inhumanity and hypocrisy — Ted whispers to himself what feels in the moment like an answer so incontestable that he remains motionless.

19. TED

On the off-ramp from the fast lane of another decade past youth and standing six-one in bare feet – he always thought the measurement accurate – a nurse claims he is actually 71 inches tall. I've shrunk an inch, Ted remarks, before figuring two. The nurse allows that such things happen while awarding him the benefit of a conceptual inch or so with her smile, but not on his medical chart.

Elsewhere, 217 elk crowding the perimeter of a winter wildlife sanctuary were (the exact phrasing: "had to be") shot, according to resident management specialists, for their own good. This amendment regarding an act of goodness undertaken in Western Wyoming, Ted hears on satellite radio while driving home from the clinic. He pictures orca herding narwhal against an Arctic shoreline before disemboweling them underwater, the mental image reconstructed from footage shot for a nature program on public television, and recalls acquaintances in human assault mode carping about other people, *those* people.

At the same hour some two thousand miles away, Gwen Sprinkles reports to the plenary session of The International Conference on Population Statistics that the date the Earth's human cohort is expected to reach 9 billion is late 2028, give or take a few weeks. She does not address the question of intolerance versus open-mindedness or how either inclination – never mind overpopulation – might be linked to broader concepts of detachment or attachment, respectively, as underlayment for the human spirit. She does not indicate what fraction of those 9 billion are likely to make decisions for their own good or the goodness of others, or how many will live their lives as labelers or the labeled.

Silencing the radio, Ted understands that words harboring temperaments laced with affect and color can trigger alarms, just as the physical shrinking of one's body pushes a hot button. Yet, when he looks up "misogyny" (synonyms: woman-hating, sexism) and "ethnophaulism" (racial slur, ethnic pejorative) that evening, he cannot summon much courage, at least not regarding the definitions themselves. This failure, he suspects, arises from the half-life of functional cortical neurons, along with the integrity of 240 trillion synapses, declining even more rapidly than his physical stature.

Rather than dwell on statistical realities that cannot readily be challenged, he wonders instead how to redress an ongoing interior wound, an anterior injury of magnitude 8+ on a scale of 10 but with external manifestations all but invisible to onlookers and his personal physician. Perhaps an expression on the lips now and then is the only giveaway, there and gone in a flash, of what? Indignation. Shame? The sensation is that of clammy skin pressing an obstacle, cognitive intention running headlong against something unyielding no one else seems to notice while conversing at the dinner table or eavesdropping in a hardware store or negotiating crowded sidewalks or scanning a friend's or family member's Facebook page. It is a feeling exacerbated by frequency of response (more accurately, nonresponse) and underwritten by 100 percent certainty about time and opportunity and physical endurance running thin.

Painful to hear from the mouth of a stranger, worse from a friend or relative who does not connect readily with the value of examined thought: there ought to be a law, Ted believes, *is* a law, of implied decency if nothing else. Yet the "F" word is again yelled at boys judged too soft or its "D" cousin at girls too hard; the "C" word gets snarled at women who speak once too often for their own good; the "N" word is muttered at "those people," thought to be stupid people and not us but somehow less than us for wanting what we want. Words never up to any good, he knows, but retained, cherished by indignant folks to use in tirades powered by overwrought limbic systems. What it does to hear such terms applied to the labeled mindlessly, if willfully, inducing a rush of blood commonly undetected from without while boiling within. What it means to observe the dark and practiced art of auditory and verbal nonchalance in The United States of America, epitomized by blather and a shrugging response along the lines: "What good would it do to say something anyway?"

As for that nephew or office worker, some runaway or the otherwise disenfranchised person of color, this is what Ted knows, really all he knows: In each verbal exchange, a thing is said while much remains unsaid dead center. Days, years pass failing expression as unused time and opportunity run out.

"Sir," he had once heard from someone – himself as well – as preface to a dialog, meaning *listen to me: there is something I must tell you*. But despite efforts to alleviate the drought, a flood of intention sublimates, leaving behind a dry streambed littered with sticks and stones and damaged bones.

20. ALI AND TED

Despite the inexcusable hour, neighbors rejoice at the racket from an exterminator van pumping poisonous cocktails into a building local news hounds would have little difficulty recognizing. From one side of the mobile unit on which a mammoth bedbug is painted, a caramel-colored hose spills through an aperture to snake onto pavement and trail across the sidewalk. Beyond an open entry and up one flight of stairs leading to a door marked 2C, a portly man in coveralls removes a half-mask N95 respirator and guides the supply line back out to the street.

Across the pavement, a passerby pauses at the café cum bakery. The man seems to stare into the distance as daylight advances to gold and a woman waves a panicky arm at the exterminator, now curbside, as if to flag him down though he is not ready to leave the scene. She yanks the front of a floral blouse to expose her midriff and points to several silver-dollar-size welts, red and unyielding to the touch. She yells above the din.

"Do these look like bedbug bites to you?"

The exterminator tilts his head an inch before responding and toggles to the "off" position the compressor switch and pump. A mechanical roar reverberates and fades.

"No, lady. You might ought to see a doctor though."

Apartment 2C, in which a single invertebrate no longer writhes, is the location to which forensic investigators had been dispatched the previous week for several purposes, including identification of a "foul odor" (reported by residents inside the building along with some neighbors across the street), subsequently determined to be cadaverine, a chemical with the composition $C_5H_{14}N_2$ recognized by the informed for its mephitic aroma as one of several benign byproducts of decaying organic matter. In the case of 2C, decaying matter sloughing from a human corpse. That of an 83-year-old mother bedridden for years. Cared for by her single son. Or so acquaintances assumed, but, in fact, left to starve on her mattress then stew for weeks in her own – as TV reporters applied the euphemism – "filth."

It is this scene Ted drives past, a slice of human history he misses. Now the pedestrian enters the modest neighborhood bakery that is flush with the fragrance of oven goods and angles toward the take-out counter, squeezing sideways between close-set tables where several loners stare at smartphones and a pair of roughnecks hunch over coffee mugs. The new customer is a young man, neither handsome nor unattractive but shorter than average and possibly of slender build, although the galabeyah hand-sewn by his grandmother obscures details of his physique. The coffee drinkers mumble an exchange in disagreeable tones that he either cannot – or prefers not to – encode. He places his order at the counter as one of the seated men questions the other at a volume none in the vicinity can fail to hear.

"He's prime, that one, Hal. Ain't that prime?"

"Pure-breed idiot knows all about camel poop. Knows how to smear camel poop on that dress of his and make it all fancy."

"Got the nose for it though." The tough guys snicker.

After settling the tab and collecting his takeaway, the young man must pass en route to the door the same table. The beefier of the two seated individuals feigns a yawn and extends both legs into the aisle.

"What's your problem there, sweetheart?"

The young man clutches the takeout, his expression that of someone abruptly returned to planet Earth after a starship journey. He shakes his head as if to clear airspace and steps over the heckler's crossed ankles.

"Sir, I don't have a problem."

"Hear that? He don't have a problem 'cept for the big attitude. Ya catch that judgy tone, Hal?"

"Damn hostile for a camel lover."

As the door closes behind his back, unfiltered sunlight breaks the horizon to assault the exiting customer's retinas. He is startled by a backfire from the exterminator van as it departs but interprets the sound as an explosion, which, in turn, conjures the struggles his parents faced in their arid homeland, one step ahead of turmoil that could take a turn for better or worse, good or evil, with no apparent logic. He half encodes disembodied voices – collective moans and snarls – of the city that is now home, and his heart thuds not at coercions implicit in moments past or present but with expectation of something ahead that drives him down the sidewalk as if demons were in pursuit or a savior beckons from the future. After racing across intersections, he rotates a key in a lock. Bounding up the stairs two at a time, he unlocks an apartment door that swings wide to admit strains of Puccini's soprano aria, "*In questa reggia*," from a pre-recorded radio broadcast.

His pulse does not settle as he sinks into a chair. Now. In this place. Ali leans toward the computer monitor and opens an AutoCAD file to access work in progress. Now. Breath comes faster at the thought of what he is plotting, dangerous imagery that has charged his spirit since leaving the apartment minutes before – or, truly, since awakening to the predawn promise of light – an ongoing mission inviting blood to surge under the skin.

Only this matters now: not the rest, neither insult nor retribution. One conceit carries meaning today. An explosive idea.

The image on the monitor fires his imagination as it morphs into a three-dimensional structure. It is an undertaking worthy of mental and emotional focus because, perhaps, no one has imagined its like before this morning. He greets his partly formed innovation as a friend in the making, organic architecture as art in celebration of humankind, half resident in computer memory and half still evolving in his mind. A breathtaking construction edges toward realization with each stroke on the keyboard, each manipulation of a mouse reaffirming originality as an enterprise that warrants passion in an arcane world. A building no bug could enter and in which no one innocent might ever die. A good place, a good palace.

21. TED

Despite annual changes to his medical insurance – increasing deductibles and decreasing coverage limits accompanied by skyrocketing premium costs – Ted still sees the primary care physician he's consulted for a decade. The one who advocates lettuce and calls his patient Theodore while staring at a laptop and rarely looking up. Ted finds a seat in the reception room and squirms for the wait, but this time he's remembered to bring his own reading material. It's a short piece that appears to be an essay about cells. Ourselves perhaps, and monsters too.

Bio You
Pinpoints of protein tadpole a collision course to dally in the dark with a dollop of idioplasm. Mated helices realign in a unicell: one micro-you.

What if I say the smallest you will ever be, micro-you, understands the language of the universe? Mathematics. Intuits geometric progression with a common ratio of two. As in

2, 4, 8, 16, 32, 64, 128,...

to 37 trillion. Understands sphericity, invagination of a layered gastrula, biconcavity of red blood, performs three-dimensional wizardry by folding proteins from random coils with expertise computational connoisseurs cannot comprehend. Orchestrates sonic hedgehog shaping in a notochord that will form a nervous system.

Knows how to build a brain.

Knows more than neurosurgeons who don't know how to build the brain you build, more than electricians the wiring of 2 billion neurowires you wire, more than any engineer or chemist how to transport through 60,000 miles of conduit the oxygen you transport and how to dispose the carbon you dispose. Understands neuroplasticity and the knitting of wounds without sutures. Appreciates through a wink of genes light as vision without Newton's help, sound as harmony sans Beethoven's legacy, and a summer's day or midsummer night with or without Shakespeare.

Genius micro-you. Expert in expression. Flawless in nuance.

Unaware now of what you knew back then, BioYou knows it nonetheless. Unaware even of awareness itself, a spark kindled awareness from unawareness then focused awareness onto sensation, brought sensation to attention, and tuned attention into perception. BioYou constructed constructs.

Beauty. Affiliation. Love.

The body shakes itself silly and calls it laughing, expels a pinch of salt in a droplet of seawater and calls it crying. The heart welcomes another vessel of life in ecstasies of passion; the head learns to despise the alien-other as heartless. Muscles tremble in fright or mobilize for flight or fight. BioYou spawns opinions.

What if I say this is how the trouble begins? Opinions welcome welcome reinforcement while dismissing the rest.

Voila! Belief.

Review, recite, repeat.

Conviction.

Monsters stir. Enemies I.D. themselves through pigmentation that is not-us. Demons arise from poverty and foreign soil, saviors from demons on home and alien turf. Guns don't kill people because they don't, and they do kill people because they do. Evolution's hokum because it is, or is not, because it isn't. Head and hardened hearts collude to reimagine war as heroic, celebrate plunder as profit, label love between men abomination and between women perversion, whereas our love is genuine love because it's ours. Aversions are picked and picked at again as if open wounds that would never mend if disavowed while convictions reinforce bias at the expense of history gone dark. Because history never happened. Or it did. Didn't it?

I could tell you living, then, is a wormhole bridging polar limits of knowing. Opposite knowings? The micro-self doesn't know it knows the constellation of ontogeny. BioYou thinks it knows humanity but doesn't know it does not know. Ample cause to stop believing everything it thinks is true is true?

Ask the unicell. Gastrula, notochord, body, head, and all.

Each expends time at subjective speed until BioYou sheds hair and smoothness, skirmishes within, and at last bequeaths to the universe:

> a poem perhaps,
> those mutual funds,
> echoed moans and
> a heap of bones.

Then again, imagine if BioYou mirrored the brilliance of micro-you.

★

Ted closes the page and allows himself to imagine.

PART FOUR

22. TED, YEARS LATER

It must have been a weekend morning when he peeked from the kitchen doorway to catch the expression of an ordinary day soon to be elevated. Likely a weekend because the waffles served by his father invited more talk than usual that day. Something to do with a relative, life and loss, then just that fast a car ride to the outskirts where in the distance a concrete high-rise layered with silver glass sliced the sky beyond a wheat field. While passing the gate with its two letters – capital vee, capital aay – and not a single tree in sight, his mother's his father's voices melted until the car pulled to a stop apart from every other vehicle but near some wires spanning high-voltage towers. How the experience began that day so long ago: waffles with honest maple syrup, better clothes for the car in case they should run into somebody along with a change in the quality of sound, and occasional sunshine for the journey under rhythmic Midwestern clouds with the sun acting shy the way a schoolteacher's nose peeks at intervals from behind a rippling stage curtain, all anticipation. Reminiscent of his father walking in the door after a long day on the base.

"Honey?" What she called her boy, Ted, at age six.

"Honey, when your father comes home at night…"

This is how she put it that summer, at age six, "... well, the thing is... don't run up to him the way you do." Her expression as forced as the tone. "Stay back a little instead of dashing out..."

Expecting to be picked up, she meant. Or nestled in his lap where each turn of the page reinforced the hybrid scent of evening-edition newsprint and fatigue. Don't joke or jump around or make noise. Leave your father alone, she meant, together with three unspoken messages that sent a stabbing sensation through the chest. That a mother *could* not say what she intended. A father *would* not say anything at all. A son must honor the warning, the order, though lacking words to express how it felt.

It. To be distanced. To discover that some expressions of love are unwelcome.

And now, in memory, the talk resumes from the front seat of the parked car. "Stop interrupting." Mother warns Father in this way when Father is not saying anything, but he lets it go because everyone knows it is just her nerves today. Undoing pickles wrapped in waxed paper to keep the sandwiches dry, she turns around with an apologetic wink while handing her two boys their lunch because no one had been interrupting anybody. Nerves and something about death or dying as she passes him his sandwich too and pecks his cheek, meaning it's okay now, and slams the passenger door to scurry toward the building with rows of glass layered high, as her auburn hair and shoulders bounce to clip-clop heels on pavement.

The three left sitting in the car hear fizzing testimony that they are beyond range, reception left down the road or tangled in wires overhead. Sorry boys no radio program today, so young Ted lowers a window and inhales aromas of ripening semi-rural biology and notices an embankment with a ditch and hint of trickling water that beckon a boy to beg please can we go see. Can we please? Yes go see, kids, but stay within sight on this nothing afternoon that, considered retroactively, after decades, is a day of which there is no finer from crib to casket. Not that that much happened during those two or three hours, except for the best in life to a seven-year-old on a partly overcast afternoon with clearing on the horizon.

Seven decades later, Ted rarely remembers where he left his shoes five minutes ago but can reconstitute in high definition the features of that childhood morning and afternoon. A plinking of percolating coffee heard from the pillow, aftertaste of real syrup from a farmer's maples, flickering sunlight on the joyride highway beyond the limits and back again into town during a round trip to some electrical towers. He knows now that the VA hospital, planted in a wheat field only months before that visit, would harvest over the years lost battles with illness, including his mother's father's alcoholism-induced cirrhosis – adults only allowed inside to comfort spent warriors, his grandfather among them – but what he remembers exactly is his father fiddling with the radio before giving up and joining Ted and his older brother outside twirling on the embankment, his father pulling from an overcoat three straws and a bag of pinto beans.

"Grab a handful, boys. Put them in your pocket."

Replays the contest invented on the spot of who can shoot a bean over the wire, lowest wire, middle, highest; two sons and their father taking turns. Better than a new comic book, cowboy movie, day pass for a Ferris wheel. He studies his father's cheeks – five o'clock shadowy despite a morning razor – as the big chest expands and lips force a puckered *thuut* and a bean goes flying at the wire in a parabolic trajectory just shy of the mark and down into the ditch of moist loam where renewal is possible a stone's throw from the dying. The afternoon a dazzling departure from workdays on the military base when his father would return too drained and unavailable to dispense affection from his chair. Recalls that whooping afternoon with longing for what happened over a lifetime and nostalgia for what never did. Regretting the things that did not develop. Did *not*. Hot-air ballooning. Summer flings in Paris, Barcelona. Trekking Amazonia before rainforests disappeared, so recalls instead a time near a wheat field removed in time and experienced as trivial at the time, but anything but trivial, looking back.

What he kept expecting in life – as though a prospect were a right – was something remarkable, rare. Something *more*. And now, having lived them, Ted understands that were he to redo any decade or every one, he would recognize that day – its destination somewhere shy of urban sprawl where pinto beans flirt with a wire – as pure gold.

END

ACKNOWLEDGEMENTS

The following chapters, some with modifications for this book, were first published in literary journals or reviews. Chapter 1, "Shirley and Her Cookie Monster," in *Sediments Literary-Arts Journal* (Issue 5, 2015); Chapter 3, "The Whole True–False, Should–Shouldn't Clifford Paradox," in *Riding Light Review* (Vol. 1, Issue 1, Summer 2014); Chapter 4, "Loving Arms," in *Shout Out UK* (May 17, 2014); Chapter 6, "Syncopation," in *The Milo Review* (Vol. 1, Issue 3, Winter 2013); Chapter 7, "Lowdown on Potatoes," in *The Examined Life: A Literary Journal of the University of Iowa Medical School* (Vol. 4, No. 1, Fall 2014); Chapter 9, "Carry-On Violation," in *Sharkpack Poetry Review Annual* (Issue 2015), a Pushcart Prize and Best of the Net nominee for 2016; Chapter 11, "Troublesome Lines Between the Lines," in *Arlington Literary Review* (Issue 76, 2015); Chapter 14, "Reverse Engineering," in *Tallow Eider Quarterly* (Winter Issue, 2015); Chapter 16, "Affidavit," in *The Blotter* (March, 2013); Chapter 19, "Sublimation by the Numbers," in *Dark Matter Journal* (Issue 7, Summer 2015); Chapter 20, "Passion at Daybreak," in *Crossways Magazine* (Ireland, Autumn 2018).Chapter 21, "BioYou," in *Eastern Iowa Review* (Summer, 2016), Experimental Fiction Prize finalist; and Chapter 22, "Shooting the Wire," in *Arts & Letters* (Issue 33, Fall 2016).